LEGACY

J Leonard Costner

Legacy Universe Publishing LLC

ISBN-13: 979-8-9889620-4-5 (EPUB)
ISBN-13: 979-8-9889620-0-7 (Paperback)
ISBN-13: 979-8-9889620-1-4 (Hardback)

Cover design by: J Leonard Costner
Library of Congress Control Number: 2023915733
Printed in the United States of America

XII IV III

CONTENTS

"Because your own strength is unequal to the task, do not assume that it is beyond the powers of man; but if anything is within the powers and province of man, believe that it is within your own compass also."

MARCUS AURELIUS, 16TH EMPEROR OF ROMAN PEOPLE

CHAPTER 1: LUKE

I 've never been afraid of Death. You could even say that I sought after our encounter. The things I've always excelled in the most have always brought me the closest to my demise. Perhaps there's someone in death that seeks me? My story may seem hard to believe, but it's true. To understand, I'll have to start from my beginning so that you will understand who I am in the end. Let's begin with my introduction; I am Luke Hart.

For as long as I can remember, I have struggled with trying to find my identity. What I do know is that I was born in America to James and Elizabeth Hart. But, beyond my birthplace and parents' names, I know nothing extraordinary about my life. The most real things I know outside my foundation are my dreams. I can't remember the last time I had a typical night's sleep.

Two dreams, in particular, have been reoccurring for months now, so vivid I can tell you every single detail, right down to the taste of the air. The first is of a woman. She calls me to her and the passion that exudes from her lips when we kiss. She smells of the sweetest flowers, her skin like satin, and her lips taste like pure candy and a miracle. Yet, if there were ever words to paint her likeness, I would silence my tongue in fear that what I would say would ruin a masterpiece and describe her as is, a dream.

I don't know who she is--maybe a figment of my imagination, a wish I so long to come true. Or is she a foreshadowing of love to come? While such bliss is a blessing, knowing that our time is limited to my slumber breaks my heart. Yet, ironically, during these bittersweet encounters, I never sleep better.

The second dream is much different. I am standing on a sandy pitch in front of thousands of screaming people. They are cheering for me as if in the worship of a god. I can't make out the name they call me or even my location, but the roar the crowd ignites as soon as I salute them is palpable. Before long, it dies away to nothing but a whisper.

A fog rolls in, and the sky begins to rain warm rose petals that kiss my skin on their way to the ground. I catch a few. The petals don't stay intact--they begin to melt, and soon I'm almost entirely submerged in a warm pool of blood. As it rolls over my face, I can no longer hold my breath. Overwhelmed, I accept the inevitable: As I am drowning, I wake up.

When I die in my dreams and awaken to the world, it's like being born again. But being born repeatedly makes you lose sight of who you are. Maybe I never really knew.

My father, "Sergeant," as I often call him, was in the army, which makes me an army brat. He wasn't so hard on me in enforcing protocol and discipline because I didn't need it.

He worked hard and was busy, so I never got to see him as much as I wanted growing up. When he was home, we had a pretty decent relationship, but my parents were young when they had me and are still very much in love. So, I never felt I was a priority for them. He spent his downtime mainly with her.

To say my mother is diligent would be an understatement. She is a successful graphic designer who managed to expand her business as we migrated.

She tried to do the stay-at-home Stepford Wife thing but quickly got bored with that role. My father was always on base or missions, and I was at school most of the day. So, she needed to fill her time, and of course, daytime TV and cleaning didn't cut it, primarily since she had nothing to clean because the house was still spotless from the day before, and morning soap operas are hard to get into when you can't speak the language of the show you're watching.

Being an only child was hard for me. I was generally alone most of the time. I had no one to talk to other than my mom and dad, although they never could quite understand what I was going through. I've lived in six countries and gone to fifteen different schools.

I was a bit of an introvert, the only one around my age who spoke English, and from early on noticed that I was different. I was never an All-American Guy. When I reached my teens, I looked more like and had the attitude of a bad boy: dark brown hair, lean muscular build, a few tattoos--I had a lot of misguided aggression.

I was really into sports. I love my competitive nature, but my knack for, and inclination toward, fighting separated me from others as a child. I have above-average gifts--exceptional strength, acute reflexes, balance, tremendous instinct, and a high IQ. Why? I don't know.

It could be genetics, but while my parents had their talents, their abilities pale compared to mine. I used to think maybe I was an alien or a mutant, you know, like the characters you read about in comic books. Perhaps I had been sent to Earth by my actual biological parents to be saved while our distant home planet was under attack and destroyed. Whatever the deal was, I embraced my gifts and mastered them.

I learned some combat skills from my dad. First, he showed me some hand-to-hand techniques the army used to train soldiers. Then, when I was eleven years old, I began formally training in mixed martial arts. For six years, I practiced hard and honed my ability, but there was something still missing. I can't recall how, but I found myself competing in organized fighting events--the unsanctioned kind.

These offered quick money, large purses, and a rush every time I stood toe to toe with a would-be opponent. But I was good at it. It brought me out of my shell and made me comfortable being around people. It also allowed me to see these foreign countries from an entirely different perspective.

The bouts were run by the shadiest of people, drug dealers, criminals, people looking to make a quick buck, and a lot of it. They accommodated business people, lawyers, and high-ranking officials, as well as criminals like themselves, people with money who had more than enough to throw around and were major fight fans with even bigger gambling addictions.

Alas, when you're dealing with sketchy characters in even sketchier environments, you're bound to run into a few dilemmas. And, I ran into a big one.

It all started when I defeated the number-one-earning fighter in Rome. A drug lord named Edmond Cross, who held ownership over the number one spot on Interpol's top-ten most wanted list, owned this fighter. When I won, Cross lost and lost big. I left the guy I fought mangled and dazed. Cross was out something like two hundred thousand dollars American if I figured the exchange rates right. At the time, I held an underground fighting record of 29-0.

I wasn't a criminal by any means, just a kid who felt alone and liked to fight. I was just caught up mingling with the wrong crowd. It came with the territory when you did what I was doing.

For my protection, the Sergeant applied for reassignment Stateside and was granted the transfer. My parents were surprisingly thrilled, seeing how, until then, they'd never taken much interest in my extra-curricular activities. We had never packed so fast to move anywhere. Before I knew it, we were on our way back to the U.S. Landing at Newark airport, I couldn't help wondering how to maintain my sanity in the Garden State. How does one go from living in Europe to living in New Jersey?

The most noticeable difference is the culture. Europeans exude a sense of place unparalleled by anything American. Every country that I had lived in owned who they were--traditions, history, social values. In America, you will find people who are proud to be American. Still, it's impossible to have a single identity because many different types of Americans call this country home. The one thing that makes the country great is the same reason it's divided.

It took some time to adjust, but it turns out New Jersey isn't so bad, I guess. We've moved to a quiet middle-class town that was very diverse. Old Town is like something out of a black-and-white television show. The houses all sit on lots with well-manicured lawns, white picket fences border the properties, and every neighbor knows the others' names. At first, my parents enrolled me in private school, thinking that it would keep me out of trouble. All it did was waste a trimester's worth of money; I registered in the local public school mid-year. Fighting was automatic grounds for expulsion; go figure. I didn't fit in there from day one. There was no way I was wearing a blazer and khakis every day.

Having just turned eighteen in my mid-junior year, I once again found myself a new student. That made the count of new schools eighteen. I transferred to the public high school in the town my parents and I lived in and found it a little more my speed. There was a wide range of people there. They were interested only in partying and dreading life after high school. You could sense the teenage angst in the air! Once I felt it, I knew I was home.

My first day of school was the day I met McKenna. They say you can, at any point, pick your head up, take a quick look, and recognize true love, love at first sight, archaic and fanciful. Today, people are led to believe that personal encounters are no longer the way to find love. You need to first have background checks, preferably with three references and a bachelor's degree. If you're still in high school, you shouldn't believe in love at all because it's too tedious. Just hook up and settle for someone who is an excellent business merger when the time's right. Who needs love? You end up getting heartbroken.

People don't realize you can't avoid life. Experiencing real heartbreak makes you stronger, and it makes finding true love so much sweeter.

You know what love at first sight is because when you see that person for the first time, the world stops, and you wonder why it seemed so meager until then. McKenna did just that for me. She was my type--five-nine, perfect skin, athletic build, captivating angelic eyes, long brown hair, and she froze time when she walked by.

You may not believe this, but it wasn't the first time we'd met. Five years ago, I met the daughter of one of the Sergeant's colleagues and best friends; like me, her father was in the armed forces. Her name was McKenna Parker. I remember this because, even at thirteen, I immediately knew she was my soul mate.

I wouldn't see her again, though, until I was seventeen. I was walking through Rome one night on my way to a fight and caught a glimpse of her hailing a taxi outside a tiny cafe. I called out to her over the bustling city sounds. I yelled until I was hoarse but failed to get her attention. I never got another chance to look for her. That last fleeting encounter happened the same night my underground fighting career caught up with me.

I couldn't stop myself from staring when she entered my first-period class. I was ecstatic to know we shared the same teacher. I've been pining over this girl, who is still a mystery to me after all this time.

"Hi, is this seat taken?" I ask.

"No, not at all!" McKenna responds. "Hey, you're new here, right?"

I smile. "Yeah. I'm Luke Hart. I just transferred from Prep. Honestly, it was more like I got kicked out."

"Really? I guess I'm going to have to watch out for you!" she exclaims while smirking at her flirtatious joke. "I'm McKenna, by the way. McKenna Parker. I just moved here too, a few months ago, from Florida. My dad got stationed to Fort Dix."

We had too much in common for this to be pure coincidence. What are the odds that we would happen to meet again in, of all places, New Jersey?

Fate has brought us together once more.

All it took was this encounter, for McKenna and I to hit it off. At the end of the school day, I walked her home. It didn't take us long to realize that we shared many similar interests--music, movies, food, even our horoscopes read. *This is one of the most heavenly matches for you because you share a near-psychic ability to communicate. At times, all you need to do is look at one another to let each other know what's up.*

McKenna's house is large and white, with dark gray tiling and a covered porch in the front of the house. I escort her up the walkway to the door. She searches through her bag until she finds her house keys. "So tell me," she asks, "how does one get kicked out of private school within three weeks of being there?"

"For fighting, if you could even call it that. The situation ended with me cleaning out my locker and a couple of star football players being rushed to the hospital with a few broken bones and minor scrapes. Nothing big!"

"So you're a fighter?" she asks with an intrigued look on her face. "I never would've guessed that. . .maybe you could show me a thing or two?" A smile crosses her face.

I knew she was the girl from all those years ago, but does she remember me? Had I left as much of an impression on her? "You don't remember me, do you? It's been five years now, but our fathers introduced us once before at a black-tie event in Paris."

She purses her lips so a dimple forms on her cheek. "Yes, I remember you. To be honest, I've always hoped I'd get a chance to see you again." She turns to enter the house.

"Wait!" I shout, reaching quickly for my cell phone. ". . .Hey, you think I could call you sometime?"

She grabs the phone out of my hand and calls hers. "Here--now you've called me some time." She smiles and slips inside.

I walk down the steps towards the sidewalk.

"See you tomorrow, Luke!" McKenna shouts from the doorway.

Lying in bed at night, I can't stop thinking about the first day of school or McKenna. I couldn't recall being so obsessed about anything in my life other than fighting.

My phone vibrates, and I have a text coming through--from *her*.

Thanks for the walk home, it reads. Wow, I guess second impressions are everything.

McKenna is still interested in me. It's time to build on that foundation. New Jersey is starting to look like a great place to be.

The following day, walking through the hallway to my first-period English class, McKenna calls to me from a distance, "Luke!....Hey, you, I wanted to know if you would do me a favor. Can I borrow your calculus book? I think I left mine at home."

"Of course!" I told her. "Hey, what are you doing Friday night?"

"Nothing, why?"

"Would you like to go out with me? Say dinner and

bowling?"

"Dinner and bowling." She smiles. "I would've thought you'd say dinner and a movie, but it's different. I like it. It's a date!"

The bell rang. Everyone in the hallway immediately stops whatever it is they are doing and head to class.

"Well, there's the bell," she says. "Guess I got to get to class. See you later?"

"Yeah, see you in class."

Friday night couldn't have come fast enough. I was so eager for it to arrive. All week I had been trying to game plan what to do during the date. It wasn't my first, but McKenna makes me nervous. I want everything to go smoothly.

I pull up to her house at 7:30 and turn off my car. The purr of my Hemi V8 engine is so loud it can wake the neighborhood. I send a text to let her know that I am outside.

I couldn't be more nervous.

We saw each other every day in school, but this

is different. This is a date. I am officially trying to take our relationship to a romantic level. If I mess up, who knows how the dynamics of our relationship will change? I have to get a grip on myself. There is no need to be nervous. She has wanted to go out with me for as long as I've wanted to with her. As long as I was myself, the person she knows and likes, nothing can go wrong.

Five minutes went by before the front door opens and I see McKenna walkout. She looks so cute-- she wore these ripped denim jeans, with a floral-patterned drop-waist cami and white flats. A perfectly tied French braid rests on her right shoulder, and she put on the sweet-smelling perfume she always wears. I can't get enough of it. Every time she is near, I get a tantalizing sensation of flowers and candy.

"Hey," she says joyfully as she enters the car, leans over, and hugs me. "So, where are we off to first?"

"Well, I figured we would go bowling first to work up an appetite and then go grab some Chinese food?"

"Nice. This is exciting. I'm excited!"

The car ride is excellent; we talk, make jokes, and

tell each other stories about our experiences. I am comfortable with her, at peace. She is genuine, and I trust her wholeheartedly.

The feeling I get from her when she looks me in the eyes can only be described as ecstatic.

Entering the bowling alley, we feel a bit out of place. There is a senior bowling league going on tonight--the elderly are everywhere.

Fortunately, we get one of the last four available lanes. As we are putting on our bowling shoes, McKenna asks me, "So why bowling?"

"Because if we were in the movies, then we wouldn't get a chance to talk, and I want to get to know you!"

"Fair enough. I hope you're ready for me. You should know I'm pretty good. Can you bowl?"

From the way her facial expression changed, I can tell that she is serious, and a competitive side of her had come along on the date. "I'm not half bad," I said. She is unaware that I love bowling and had previously learned how to spin the ball across the lane like the pros. The shadow of a smile passes over her lips.

"Well, then. I have an idea. Why don't we make this interesting?"

I laugh, knowing where this is going. "What do you have in mind?" I ask.

"If I win... if I win, you have to be my personal slave for a month!" That doesn't sound too bad to me.

"Deal. And what happens when I win?"

"If you win, you get whatever you want!"

She seems certain of her skill, so I accept. I take a second to think about what it is that I want. There is only one thing: a kiss. It's said that you can tell everything you need to know about a person from the first kiss. I knew she was perfect; I want to see if my feelings are on target. "If I win, I want you to kiss me."

"Well, I guess you won't be getting a kiss tonight, then!"

Six strikes and four spares later, it was time for me to collect. I can't help but laugh. McKenna has an angry look on her face.

"What's wrong?" I ask, grinning from ear to ear.

"I hate to lose. You hustled me! I'm not half bad. What was it with the pro spin?" she demands.

"I'm sorry if you feel misled by my modesty. I guess you can say bowling is a hobby of mine."

"Whatever." She grabs me double fisted by my shirt and kisses me. It was the most incredible kiss of my life. Our lips pursed together, locked in a passionate, breathtaking moment.

We unhook slowly and pull away from each other, gazing into each other's eyes, our expressions conveying the same message, amazed at how perfect that kiss was. Neither one of us wanted to ruin it by saying something stupid.

"Um... ready to eat?"

Still speechless, she nods, grabs my hand, and leads the way back to the car.

I took her to a new Chinese place called the Asian Bistro, a modern restaurant and the perfect intimate place for a first date. We sat on the outside patio, surrounded by stands of bamboo and illuminated by strings of star-like lights. There is a large hanging lamp, off-centered in the shape of a white paper ball, that looks like the moon.

Usually, in this part of Jersey, stars can't be

seen because of the ambient light. But that night, right through the simulated starry night, they made a special appearance. As if the moment couldn't have gotten any better, music starts playing in the background.

"This is one of my favorite songs," McKenna says. "When I first heard it, I knew it would always be the background music to my dreams.

I would play this and imagine dancing to it with someone who would make the moment just right."

"Care to dance?" I ask, hoping I can make that dream come true. I extend my hand across the table. McKenna takes it, and I escort her to the dance floor. She places her right hand in mine, her left arm drapes over my shoulder, and her head rests on my chest. We slow-dance to the perfect moment—nothing else in the world matters.

McKenna looks up at me smiling, with a moist sheen in her eyes, and says, "Thank you."

I swear the last two years of my high school experience were like an '80s movie montage. Days started to mesh together, and time was flying faster than ever. In two weeks, we became a couple, and I loved every second. I could have sworn John Hughes was directing my life.

She kept me out of trouble, and I showed her a few fighting techniques. She is a natural. I couldn't have wished for anything more.

Before I knew it, we had graduated and were on our way to college. McKenna and I were both accepted into Yale. I didn't think it suited my personality, but wherever McKenna was, that's where I was going to be.

I continued to train as hard as I had while I was still in Rome. Despite not having been in an actual fight since I was in Europe, I can't begin to explain to you how much I longed for it. Not the whole part about nearly being killed by a sore- loser drug lord, no, but I missed the rush I got from testing my ability against someone who was set on destroying me. I guess I hadn't felt truly challenged in a while. I was itching to get a fight--and soon.

CHAPTER 2: THIS MIGHT NOT BE SO BAD AFTER ALL!

I 've only been at school for four weeks, and boredom is already starting to set in. Don't get me wrong--I love that McKenna and I are together. It's a great school too as far as academics, very prestigious, but I can't take the dull atmosphere anymore. There isn't much to do here. Maybe for a person who is from New Haven, Connecticut, it is different.

As far as the campus goes, Yale is astonishing. The buildings exude history; they remind me of Hogwarts. I decided to major in Business. Since I was already good at making money, I figured that I might as well get a degree in it. Besides, Yale is ranked in the top 20 business programs in the country. I would be a fool not to pursue a degree from here.

I am on course to graduate in precisely four years, assuming I could last that long. To be honest with you, I am not sure I can stick it out. People go to college to earn a degree to have a better chance of getting a good job. People want good jobs to support their family, if they have one or want to start one. There is one thing I am sure I can make a living at--but as long as McKenna is still attending school, why shouldn't I go? My classes are a breeze. School has always come easy to me, but there is one class I can't stand, which is my history elective. The professor is terribly dull, and why would I want to learn about world history?

As I lope through the campus courtyard, I hear my name called. "Hey, Luke, wait up!" McKenna yells from across the quad.

"Where you off to?"

"I've got a meeting with my advisor. I need to try and get out of this history class; it's so lame. I know it's late, but I want to see if I can get assigned to another class."

"Good luck with that. Dinner tonight at 7:00?"

"Of course!"

McKenna hurries off. "Great!" She yells over her shoulder. "Love you."

I make it to my appointment with my advisor. I have been in her office for thirty minutes before she finally came around to telling me what I already knew. This woman is annoying me--the gray wool pants suit she is wearing is making her itch, and she has been involuntarily scratching herself the entire time I've been in the office. She has also been staring at me with marked disinterest. I guess she doesn't want to be here either.

"I'm sorry, Luke, but all classes are full. It's only been four weeks--why don't you give the class another shot? Who knows? Maybe by midterm, things will have turned around."

What a waste of time, I think. There's no possible way I will last till midterm.

"Please? I'm *begging* you here. Isn't there *anything* else I can take?"

"Well...there is *one* class that still has an open seat. Roman Society with Professor Shields. He just had five students withdraw from his class, so there is plenty of room."

Any other person would've wondered why so many people had dropped the class. Was it that difficult, or was he so much of a tyrant that not too many people can stand to be there? I don't care; all I know is that anything will be better than staying in World History.

I would be well-rested and failing by the time the semester is over.

"I'll take it!"

"Alright, then, I'll give you the sign-in form. Remember, you have to get Professor Shields to sign it for it to be official. You better hurry, though--the class will be starting in ten minutes on the other side of campus."

I get up and rush over.

I have never been on that side of campus, and by the time I get there, I am lost. Eventually, I find the class. When I walk in, all I hear is, "You're late. Take a seat!"

This guy is for sure no pushover. Professor Shields looks familiar to me. He is about five-ten or -eleven, has a short haircut, so you can tell he is balding. Shields is built like he religiously works out and has a British accent. I could have sworn I've seen him before.

"Who here has seen the movie, *Gladiator*? Well, unlike the Academy-Award-winning movie, with all those wonderful actors, gladiators existed and were the equivalent of today's rock stars." Shields says.

Professor Shields' lecture notes:

264 BCE during the first Punic Wars, the sons of Junius Brutus Pera offered gladiator games in honor of their recently deceased father. Munus, the commemorative right owed the deities of the loved ones' ancestors. Gladiator games became exceptionally popular. Men who offered games would compete for the number of matches to be presented.

Gladiator games continued to thrive. Days of combat would be presented in honor of anyone who had passed away. The games would turn from memorial events to money-driven proceedings in the blink of an eye. In 105 BCE, Rome gave its first showing of gladiator combat from Capua. The name is derived from the Etruscan

"Capeva."

Capua is located in southern Italy, in the province of Caserta, Campania. Businessmen tried to make a name for themselves in government by owning and putting on the best gladiator matches.

The buying, selling, and trading of gladiators became popular throughout the empire. Commonly the enemies of Rome, tribes conquered in battle, would be enslaved and sold for the games. Most were martyrs, just sent to be lambs for the slaughter. Roman society was obsessed with blood and death.

Those who were proven to be great fighters were sold as gladiators.

I have to admit that, even with Shields' warm personality', maybe this class won't be so bad after all.

The lecture is intriguing, to say the least. I had lived in Rome for two years and never took the time to research the history. For some strange reason, I feel a deep connection to the information in the lecture.

Before he can get a chance to finish, the class period is over. I am a little disappointed, but I know it is the class for me. While everyone is leaving the room, I approach Shields to sign me into the course. Before I can reach him, Shields begins to speak, "Good afternoon, Mr. Hart. I hadn't planned on seeing you so soon."

"So soon?" I wonder, trying to remember again if I had met him somewhere and how he knows who I am?

"I would be lying if I said the pleasure was all mine," I admit.

He chuckles. "You're wondering how I know you?"

I've managed to stay pretty low-key since returning to the U.S. I've only been training and focusing on my relationship with McKenna and school.

I start to get a weird vibe before he speaks again.

"Two years ago, while in Rome, I participated in a back- alley sporting event in Termini. I remember watching you fight. I heard the stories of the young American fighter who destroyed everyone who dared face him in the ring. I was impressed. I fought the French gentlemen immediately following your match."

Instantly I know who Shields is. I had watched him fight that night--a ridiculous no-contest. Shields is one of the greatest martial artists I have ever seen. The fight had lasted only a minute. He had toyed with the guy for a bit before finally landing a three-move combination that left the Frenchman looking like a coma victim. What is he doing as a college professor at Yale? It doesn't add up.

"Before you start racking your brain trying to figure out why a professor would take part in questionable activities like that, let me tell you the answer is simple: I am a fighter by nature, just as you are.

Tell me, Luke, do you still mix it up?"

"I haven't gotten the opportunity since you last saw me. My win didn't go over so well with a few people, so my family and I left Europe. I've just been staying in shape for the moment, waiting for the right place and right time. I'm always up for a good fight."

He can tell I am itching to get back into action. If it isn't apparent from my words, just the thought of competition gets me excited and brings a smile to my face. Shields is right; I am a fighter by nature.

"That's good to hear. You will soon... I believe you have something for me to sign? Let's have it." He scrawls a bold signature on the sheet. "You are now officially in my class. Don't be late next time!"

What did he mean by "you will soon?" Shields wastes no time after our talk; he is out the door before I can ask. I leave the annex and head back towards my apartment.

I feel my phone vibrate. It's McKenna. She's sent a text: *Get back here pronto. I've got something special for you to unwrap.*

The text brings a smile to my face. I always love the little innuendos. Before you get ahead of yourself, though, let's make it clear that McKenna and I have a very mature and healthy relationship.

As I finish texting back, I notice some commotion in the distance. A kid looks like he is being hassled by a sketchy group of guys. The kid looks around my age-- slim, kind of sloppy, and from the look of it, he needs a little help.

I usually try not to make it my business to interfere in the affairs of others, but I can't resist. Old memories triggered a natural urge, so I went looking for trouble.

"Gentlemen, what seems to be the problem?" I ask.

"What? Get out of here!" Barks one of the guys in the crew. He is a short, compact guy with a buzz cut that looks vaguely military.

"Hey, why don't you let him go? You all look like you have more important things to do than messing with him."

"I don't know what your *problem* is, but you are looking to get yourself worked over along with your little friend!"

"Really? I'd like to see you try."

The guy standing in front of me throws the first punch. I duck the swing and connect my fist with his face. It isn't long before I am being swarmed with goons. The incident is giving me a rush, the kind I haven't felt in a long time. They aren't bad fighters-- they are skilled and have formal training but, they are no match for me.

When it seems to be over, the outspoken guy with the buzz cut changes everything. He pulls out a short sword he has concealed in his coat.

"Overcompensating a bit?" I ask. "Whatever happened to the old switchblade? You just carry a sword around?" My attacker doesn't seem amused by my attempt at humor.

He takes two hard swings at me with the blade before I disarm him with a quick wrist twist and a right cross that knocks him out cold. The rest of the group is giving up; they collect their friend and head off. I continue to flex my knuckles as I watch them fade into the distance.

"Thanks!" the kid says.

"Don't mention it. Friends of yours?"

"No, just messengers from the House of Crassus. You're in Professor Shields' class, right?" the kid asks. "I saw you come in. I'm Bobby."

He isn't an intimidating-looking guy, just a regular-looking kid in Professor Shields' class.

"House of Crassus? What's that?"

Bobby laughs, "a guy with your talent should know about them.

Shields hasn't told you yet, has he?"

"Told me what exactly?" There is something I am

missing.

"If you have time, I can introduce you to the opportunity of your life, a fighter's dream!" Bobby offers.

I am interested to see what he is talking about. If what he is saying is true, it could be just the thing I've been looking for.

"Okay, I'll give it a shot. Not tonight though, I have to be somewhere."

"Meet me here tomorrow at 9 am. You'll want to see this."

I get back to my apartment a bit later than planned. When I open the door, I see McKenna has gone all out, setting a mood. Red and white candles are lit all around the apartment. The smell of vanilla and marshmallow peppermint fills the air. Freshly plucked rose petals are scattered over the floor, and a song she and I both love is playing on the speakers.

Is it my birthday? I can't begin to imagine what I have done to deserve this.

There is a note dangling from the light in the

hallway. The directions on it tell me to follow the arrows McKenna has laid out until I find my gift.

I began following the directions until I find myself in front of the bedroom door. I open it slowly, anticipating what I will find when I enter the room.

Once inside, I find McKenna lying across the bed, waiting for me. Her long brown hair is down, her arms stretched back, legs crossed, and she is wearing a chocolate Sunday. Whipped cream and chocolate fudge, starting from the curves of her perfectly shaped breasts, pour down her magnificently gorgeous abdomen and ended at her mouth-watering flower. As a bonus, she had even laid a cherry on top of her cherry. I look at my dessert, smiling harder than I ever have before.

It is kinky even by our standards. McKenna is a very spontaneous person, so it doesn't surprise me that she would do something like this. She has a mesmerizing look and aura. There is a restless gaze in her eyes. I can tell she has been waiting for me to come home for a while.

"What's the occasion?" I ask.

"You missed dinner, so I figured we would go straight to dessert."

That is all I need to hear. I waste no more time before I ate every inch of my treat. We make mind-blowing love and a mess of the room.

When we are done, we have to straighten out the bedding, so we can sleep. The sheets are a mess. There's whipped cream and chocolate stains all over them, and the mattress is hanging halfway off the box spring. We had a fantastic time.

That night I have the strangest dream. I am back during what looks like the Roman Empire, in the middle of an arena, standing over a dead man. I am covered in blood, holding a sword, and the people in the crowd are cheering for me.

I can't make out what they are saying. Just as I start to hear something clearly, McKenna wakes me from my sleep.

"Luke! *Luke!*"

I awake heavily, breathing and drenched in a cold sweat.

"Wow, that was too real," I tell her.

"Are you okay?"

"Yeah, I'm--I'm fine. I just had the most vivid dream. I have to go to the bathroom."

I wash my face and try to get ahold of myself. I am looking in the mirror when I notice what appears to be a new scar across my chest. I hadn't seen it before, and I'm pretty sure I would've remembered getting cut across my right pectoral.

It is too weird for me to deal with right now. I tell myself I'd figure it out later. It's already very late, and I want to make sure I meet Bobby in the morning.

9 am rolls around, and I meet Bobby, where we had parted ways the night before. We walk for a good fifteen minutes before coming to a large stone building labeled *Aurelius*. I follow Bobby down the hallways and three staircases until we come to a large, dimly lit room, the floor of which is covered in sand. Chryselephantine statues line the walls; huge lights hang from the ceiling. Large storage units at either end of the room appear to be housing antique-style weapons. Swords, spears, tridents, shields, and a few

other items I am unfamiliar with. I don't know where I am, but the room reminds me of Rome, the Coliseum, and the statues that resemble gladiators whose stories I have often heard growing up in Europe.

Bobby taps me on the shoulder, "hurry! We're missing the match!"

"What match?"

I chase after him to a balcony overlooking the room. Down below, a cheering crowd of guys has circled two men fighting with swords--and it isn't your pampas rich kid fencing. Nobody is wearing protective gear.

There is no prancing and lunging with thin rapiers. These guys are swinging genuine weapons at each other.

It doesn't take me long to recognize one of the fighters. It is Professor Shields. The guy he is fighting is very skilled. My god, I think to myself. Actual fighting, real fighters, and, oddly, the weapons added another level of intrigue I can't ignore.

I am looking forward to giving this a shot when I figure out what I am watching.

When the match ends, Bobby walks me down to the center of the crowd. "Hello, Bobby," said Shields. "Mr. Hart, you've managed to find your way to our little home away from home. Welcome to the House of Aurelius!"

I have no idea what I am being welcomed to, but I am captivated.

"All right, gents," Shields goes on, "that's enough for today. Get out of here and go do something else. We'll start at the same time tomorrow. Good day."

"What is this place?" I ask when everyone has left.

"Come with me. All of your questions will be answered," Shields assures me.

I follow him back through the halls to what I assume is his office. Outside stands a marble statue of a long-bearded old man. The caption on the sculpture reads *Marcus Aurelius*. I knew the name. I had heard it when I attended school in Italy.

"You know who this is?" Shields asks.

"Yes, Marcus Aurelius. Sixteenth Emperor of Rome."

"He was a philosopher," Shields says, "and the last

of the Five Good Emperors. A knowledgeable man and he conducted himself as such. After Nero had his way with Rome, Marcus did everything he could to restore the empire to its former glory. It was his wish to return the power of the senate to the people. A great figure of history-- which is why he's the namesake of this building."

"What is this? A fraternity?"

"Yes and no. It's not a fraternity in a sense you're thinking of. We have no affiliation with the school, we do nothing in any generous capacity, and the ordinary student population knows little to anything about us. This is not the type of place you can pledge. This is a fraternity of special people just like you—a brotherhood of warriors whose bloodlines have given them a remarkable fighting ability. The men apart of the House of Aurelius and those of rival groups descend from ancient warriors. Kings, knights, generals, gladiators, warriors--throughout history-- you can find ties to legends in this discrete world of competition. We are a part of what is called 'Legacy,' a network of, well, you can call them 'Sects,' like ours.

There are eight in total, five of which are located in the United States." He glances at me, his eyes clear and focused. Shields is trying to get a read on how I am receiving the information.

"We fight in quarterly events--real weapons, real fighters, and fatalities most certainly a possibility. Entirely legal, and those behind this are so involved it makes the back alley fights in Italy seem like public street brawls. You must have money, or a name, to be a spectator. The students you will see at these events come because their parents can afford it, and their money is as old as our world."

It isn't hard to imagine what he was saying is true. America *is* the land of opportunity. Fighting as a spectator sport has lost some of its lusters. Boxing is hanging on by a thread, and MMA has taken its place in the hearts of people. This is unlike anything in recent history. No wonder discretion is a priority since money and the possibility of death is involved. Aside from that, a question remains in my head. Where do I fit in? And why is Shields exposing it to me?

"If it's such a big secret, why are you telling me this right now?" I have to know.

Shields stops and looks me directly in the face. What he is about to tell me requires my undivided attention.

"Have you ever dreamed of glory? Imagined that you had conquered something and stood watching as people cheered for you as if you were an inspiration to them?"

How does he know I have dreams like that? Earlier, when I mentioned that I was waiting for another real fight, Shields told me I'd find one soon. Then I happen to meet Bobby, who brought me to Aurelius. Now I am being exposed to a secret society so kept under wraps that not a single outsider is permitted to know it exists.

"Let me get this straight. Are you saying you've been keeping an eye on me ever since Termini?" I inquire.

He laughs; the sound of his amusement fills the silent room. "We have been following you since *birth*. The Historian is never wrong."

"The Historian?"

Shields sighs as if he is frustrated with my ignorance. "It's the Historian's job to follow bloodlines in an effort, hopefully, to find the next great champions of Legacy. You, my friend, you are one of those champions."

I am a little creeped out and, at the same time, interested, too. Shields has my attention. If I have understood him correctly, I am the descendent of a legendary warrior.

"Okay, this is cool. Tell me more." We began walking again, and I am all ears as more is revealed to me.

"Legacy gets its name from the fighters themselves. Legacy is what it is because the fighters are just that, exceptional descendants born with the natural abilities and skills of the warriors whose names reign supreme throughout history. They fight because of this inheritance, these gifts. The blood coursing through their veins demands glory." He sucks on a tooth, pauses again, and turns to me.

"Have you noticed any new scars recently that you

can't account for?"

"Yes. Yes, I have. How do you know this?"

Shields laughs again. "The Historian never ceases to amaze me. You're an Echo. Echoes get their name because they're virtually duplicates, mirror images, doppelgangers. An Echo's blood is so in tune with its ancestor, you're practically their seed. Only four Echoes are known to Legacy.

I am one of them. Two are currently fighting in Legacy, and you are now the fourth. I am the descendent of King Richard the Lionhearted."

"Richard the Lionhearted?" I am amazed. Richard, son of King Henry II, received his name because he was revered as one of the great military leaders and warriors of English history. He commanded Christian armies during the third crusade and gave Saladin the Great a pretty good beating. I said this to Shields.

"You know your history," he replied. "That's good-- it will come in handy."

I begin to understand why, for the longest time, I have felt so different from others. It is because of my blood. My ancestor had been a great warrior, and I am their reincarnated spirit. But Shields had still not yet told me who my ancestor was.

"Who does the Historian say *I* am born of?" I ask. We are interrupted before he can answer; there is a knock at the door.

"Come in!" Shields says. When the door opens, the guy Professor Shields had been sparring with enters the room.

"Getting slow, old man!" the guy says.

"In what life, may I ask, do you imagine you could best me? Luke, I want you to meet someone. This is Lincoln."

"Call me Linc. So you're the Echo, huh? How are you doing?"

"Not bad. I saw you fighting out there. You're pretty good."

"Well, I try," he says. "I'm only going to be as good as the work I put into it."

"So nice you've made friends already," Shields says drily. "How touching! If you will excuse me, gents, I am running late for my 8 pm class."

Shields leaves Linc and me to talk.

Linc is a good guy. I immediately feel like I can trust him. He has a lean, athletic build, almost like a sprinter, and a short haircut. After speaking for a while, we become fast friends.

I have been here all day, and there is someone important I have to see, McKenna. I depart the house, knowing that it would not be the last time I step foot in there. Bobby was right when he said the opportunity of my life.

When I got back to the apartment, she is furious. "I've been going at this over and over for the past three hours, and nothing will stick."

"What's wrong?" I ask.

"I'm supposed to be working on a project for Anthro, and I can't come up with anything to write about."

"What's the project suppose to be about?"

"We have to do a study of a person and his or her lifestyle and cultural habits. The project runs through the end of the semester, and I can't figure who to focus on." McKenna is a journalism major, stressful, so she is constantly typing away in the library or at the apartment. Sometimes it is hard to find her during the day, but I support her ambition. She wants to be a writer more than anything. In high school, she was the editor of the school newspaper senior year. She used to write me little poems to tell me how much she loved me. I've read everything McKenna has ever written.

"I'll do it." I offer.

"You? Do what?"

"I'll be your subject."

"Luke, thanks, but no. While you do have a broad and wildly eccentric background, you wouldn't be a good subject. You're just a student now."

There is so much to me that she has yet to find out, so much I have just found out myself and am still gathering information on. Shields had said discretion was a priority for Legacy, but what could it hurt to tell McKenna? We didn't keep secrets from each other. "I promise you," I say, "you will not be disappointed."

"Okay, I'll do it. You better give me some good material. Before we start, though, I think we should do something *fun*. Let's go out!"

"What would you like to do? The world is your oyster."

"I don't know. I wonder what there is to *do* in this town."

I have something in mind. Earlier, when Linc and I were talking, he'd told me about a party being thrown by a member of Aurelius at a club a few blocks away from campus called Haze. The party is by invitation only, and since I will be a part of the brotherhood, an invitation had been extended to me.

"How about going to a party?" I ask. "Music, drinks, socially inept college kids?"

"Sounds good to me!" McKenna is in.

We take our time and get ready to head out. McKenna wore a fiery red exposed shoulder top, floral lace leggings, and black rhinestone suedette wedges. Her long brown hair is flowing down her back, and she wore a pair of diamond studs I had bought her for our first anniversary. McKenna always put on very little makeup because of her natural beauty.

Tonight is a special occasion, though. The contouring on her face highlights the color of her eyes. They are sparkling like Broadway lights.

I text Linc for directions to the party, and he messages me back to look for him outside the club. It took what seemed like years to get to Haze. We finally end up outside the building that is perched down a tight alleyway.

The marquee has the name of the club in neon blue set against a rectangular silver background. Two bouncers stand outside in identical black suits, and sunglasses, at midnight. We wait for five minutes outside before Linc shows up.

"Luke, what's going on, Bro?" Linc asks.

"Nothing much, man. We came to check out the party. Linc, this is my girlfriend, McKenna."

"Hey," she says.

"Very nice to meet you. This is my girl, Juliet. Juliet, Luke, and McKenna."

"Hi, nice to meet you guys," said Juliet, who is gorgeous --slim and curvy, with long dark-brown hair and a caramel complexion.

"Let's party!" Linc exclaims.

He walks up to the bouncer and says, "We're here

for the Aurelius party."

"Password?"

"Glory."

They open the doors, and we immediately hear EDM music blasting from inside. Strobing lights and lasers paint a sea of people having a good time. There are bars on every wall of a large, high-ceilinged room and a giant dance floor, with an LED lighting system controlled by a technician, in the middle. The DJ booth is in the back left corner overlooking the party, and couches and ottomans occupied both ends of the floor.

Linc navigates us through the party to the VIP section off towards the back, with another set of bouncers guarding the area.

We sat around for a while drinking, enjoying each other's company, sharing stories, and getting to know one another. Linc and Juliet seem good together. McKenna takes a liking to her. Since we have been at school, neither of us has made much effort to acquire new friends.

"So, Luke," Juliet says, "how did you and McKenna

meet?"

"Well, when we were children, our families attended the same formal event in Italy. Our fathers were colleagues. That night, they introduced us, and I fell for her as soon as I saw her. But we couldn't keep in touch, and five years went by before we saw each other again. When my family moved back to America, McKenna and I wound up in the same class, and we've been inseparable ever since. I won't lose her again."

"That's so nice!" Juliet is elated by our story.

"What about you guys?" McKenna asks.

"Linc and I... well, it wasn't anything as romantic as that. It was pretty normal, you could say."

"Normal?" Linc laughed. "We met when Juliet came to my dorm room knocking, kicking, and screaming. She was looking for this guy who had spread a rumor about them hooking up because she wouldn't go out with him. When I opened the door, she didn't even wait to see who it was--as soon as she got a clear shot, she took it, punched me square in the face, thinking that I was the other guy. When she realized that I wasn't who she was looking for, Juliet apologized profusely, invited herself in, and she's been beating me ever since!"

"Stop it!" Juliet says. "I don't beat you *all* the time."

"That's a great story," said McKenna. "You guys seem amazing together! After all of these drinks, I need to use the bathroom. Juliet, will you come with me?"

"Of course I will--give us a chance to have some girl time. We'll be back. Don't miss us too much, boys."

They head off. Bobby shows up almost immediately after they are out of sight.

"What's going on, guys?"

"How are you living?" Linc asked.

"I can't complain. How's the party? Any fine ladies around in need of some loving?"

I laugh, "I wouldn't know, big guy. We've been entertained by our fine ladies. I'm sure there are few out there who have your name written all over them, though."

"You're probably right. I'm going to chill with my boys first before I make my move. You know what I mean, homies?"

"You got it. Hard not to like you, man." Linc says.

"So, Bobby," I say, "if you don't mind me asking, how did *you* get linked up with Aurelius?"

"Well, I don't have the physical abilities you guys do, but I'm better looking... And I have something else important that's essential to the house. I'm the Historian!"

"You?"

"Well, okay, so I'm not technically the Historian for Aurelius. I'm in training. My father is the actual Historian. He is the one that discovered you and has been following your progression since birth. I'll take over when he retires. My family has been Historians for generations.

I'll be the sixth generation."

"Wow, that's cool, man." It's still a bit weird thinking that something so elaborate as this clandestine world has been going on for hundreds of years, and no one has ever even heard of it outside of the people who are allowed in.

"So, how much has Shields told you so far?" Bobby asks me.

"Just a bit about Legacy and the Echoes. He had to run before I could get any more information from him."

"Legacy is the coolest thing of all time. It is the time of the Gladiator in a modern setting. The fighting continued when Rome declined, you know--the blood ran on.

To be able to fight, you have to be a Bloodborn. Those are the ones who have original bloodlines to warriors of the past. The Echoes, like you, are doppelgangers. You are, skill-wise and physically, almost identical reincarnations of your 'Origins,' as we call them, with slight variations. There are also Relics, Bloodborn whose families have maintained the traditions of their ancient cultures. They live by the same codes, pray to the same gods. You get it."

"Wait, so you can tell me who my Origin is, right?" I figure he should know. Suddenly, a ruckus breaks out by the bar. I look towards the commotion and notice two guys starting trouble with McKenna and Juliet.

"What's up?" Linc asks.

"I don't know yet." I hop over the wall that is

sectioning off the VIP lounge and race over. The crowd has formed a circle, and the music has stopped. Everyone is watching what is going on.

"I thought I told you to get *lost,*" I hear McKenna snarl. "Touch me again, and I'll snap your fingers until they all break one by one."

"She is feisty. I like that," the guy she is addressing said to the other before turning back to the girls. "Why don't you let me work out some of that aggression?"

"Let's just go," said Juliet, grabbing McKenna's elbow and turning to walk away.

Just then, the guy touches McKenna's shoulder. She turns and thrusts her palm up into his nose and, as he is falling backward, grabs his index finger and breaks it. "That's the first one," she says in an ominously low voice. "There's four left."

"You broke my *finger!*" He tries to backhand McKenna, but before he can bring his arm forward, I finally manage to slip through the crowd and hit him with a two-move combination that puts him on the ground. I gave his friend a head kick to the temple just for good measure.

The crowd is stunned. I don't think what I just did is that impressive, but they are moved to silence.

I turn to check on McKenna. Linc is right behind me with Juliet.

"Are you okay?" I ask.

"Yeah, just dealing with creeps."

"Hey, you! Not bad; you took them out pretty swiftly. How about you try one more time with me?"

Whispers start to float through the crowd as I hear someone challenge me to a fight. I turn to find a tall, broadly built man standing in front of the two guys I had just laid out.

He is six-four, with shoulder-length hair. He is easily 230 pounds of pure muscle and has a deep, menacing voice. I can see why everyone went silent. I don't know who this person is, but it is obvious everyone else does. I've never backed down from anyone, and he wasn't about to be my first.

"No problem," I say, accepting the offer.

The guy and I are standing directly in front of one another when someone steps in between us. He is a lean, curly-haired man of slightly more than average height and who seemed to command the room's attention without so much as a raised voice.

"What are you doing here, Owen?" he asks, his eyes riveted on the man.

"Nikko. Pleasure as always."

"I asked you a question. What are you doing here? You Crassus swine are not welcome on Aurelius property."

"Rumor has it you have a new member. An Echo? Judging from the condition of these two, I take it this little runt is the one."

"Whether he is or not is no concern of yours. If I were you," Nikko added, "I would leave the premises immediately."

"All right, we're leaving. But, you and I," Owen says, turning to address me, "will see each other again. History always repeats itself."

I nod and smile. Clenching my jaw the entire time Owen is leaving the building, regretting that we weren't able to have it out.

I wanted to destroy the guy, whoever he was. He seems to frighten people. I wonder why? If all these guys are born fighters, why were some so hesitant to defend their club?

"I don't believe we've had the pleasure of being formally introduced, Luke. I'm Nikko. Welcome to the party."

"Who was that guy?" I ask.

"That, my friend, was Owen, the top Crassus fighter. He thinks he's a god. Don't worry about him, though. I'll personally take care of Owen. We are due to meet in the Proelium, and I guarantee he will not walk away unscathed. Come on, let me get you a drink."

He shows us back to the VIP section and has a hostess bring us refreshments. Once we are seated, Nikko leaves us to resume his obligations as host.

"Whoa, that would've been epic if those two squared up just now," Bobby declared.

"Why do you say that?" I ask.

"Do you know who that *is*? That is Owen of Crassus, the Echo of Achilles himself. Can you say 'hardcore stuff'? Owen has a god complex because Achilles was rumored to have been a demigod--not to mention

Owen's never lost a fight in Legacy."

I very much doubt he is a demigod, although Achilles was a true warrior. Achilles was the son of the nymph, Thetis, who is said to have dipped Achilles in the waters of the river Styx to make him immortal. She submerged everything but his heel, the only vulnerable spot on his body. *Hercules,* the son of Zeus, was a demigod, but Achilles? I don't know. I can't take anything away from his Origin, but I have a hard time believing that Owen is him.

"The beef between Nikko and Owen goes back to ancient times. Nikko is the descendent of Hector, prince of Troy. You know the story; everyone does. Hector's brother Paris ran off with Helen, the wife of Menelaus, King of Sparta. He was so pissed that he, and his brother Agamemnon, King of Argos, assembled a fleet of over a thousand ships to sail on Troy. Agamemnon was a power-hungry tyrant who spared no expense in his mission.

He brought Menelaus, Ajax, Odysseus, and Achilles. Achilles didn't even want to fight--he had ordered his men, the Myrmidons, to sail away from Troy.

But, they followed him into battle because of a misunderstanding, unaware that their leader wasn't Achilles but instead his cousin Patroclus. Hector met Patroclus in battle and killed him. In a blind rage, Achilles marched on the gates of Troy, where he and Hector faced off *mano a mano*. Hector put up a pretty good fight, but in the end, he fell to Achilles' blade." Bobby explains.

"Before the whole Trojan Horse fiasco and the sacking of Troy, Hector's wife Andromache escaped the city with their infant son Astyanax. Thus, the bloodline lived on. What people don't know, and what history doesn't tell, is that Briseis, the cousin of Hector, also escaped with Andromache that day. She was a mythical queen, captured and given to Achilles as a war prize. She ended up falling for the guy, and they made sweet love. Their nights of passion resulted in the conceiving of a child. When people started noticing her baby bump, everyone assumed the father was Briseis' husband. He had been killed, along with their family, when the Myrmidons assaulted Troy. In actuality, it was Achilles' kid.

Briseis knew that the baby wasn't from her dead husband, but she could never tell anyone the truth. The baby wouldn't have survived in the fallen city. Only when the child reached his manhood did she confide in him the truth of his birth."

"How do you know all of that?" I ask. Bobby has a wealth of knowledge.

"Duh, I'm a Historian, remember? Besides, Achilles was the greatest fighter the world had ever seen. Of course, his blood would maintain the instinctual need for mayhem."

Forgive me, but I am not swayed by that history lesson. Immortal, he wasn't. Gods don't die, and if he was so great, why did he meet his end in Troy? Owen may have been of Achilles' bloodline, but he was just a man like everyone else. I was looking forward to Nikko and Owen fighting for real. But if I got the chance to demolish him first, I would wipe up the floor with him.

McKenna knew it had taken a lot for me to not fight him there and then. I needed a distraction, and she knew exactly what to do. She grabs my hand, looks at me, and gives me a suggestive smile. We had a connection so strong it was almost telepathic. She rises out of her seat and pulls me to the middle of the dance floor. She throws her arms around me and says, "it's just you and me tonight."

CHAPTER 3: LET'S GEAR UP!

I have been training at Aurelius for three straight weeks, and I'm starting to get anxious. My hand-to-hand defense and striking are still unmatched, but I have been working with different weapons, trying to get a feel for them. Since these battles require more than a free wielding motion, the technique is most important to be effective with a weapon.

"Have you not chosen your *weapon* yet?" Shields had started to get annoyed.

"I don't know which one to choose."

"It's not that hard a choice. If it is meant to be, the weapon will almost choose you. You will know which is yours by the way it feels when you wield it."

I don't know what he wants me to do. I stare at the weapons for a minute before I lock my eyes on the sword. I pick it up and have a different feeling as I am holding it.

"I think this is it," I said. As I turn, I see Shields swing his blade at my head as if he is trying to decapitate me. I quickly block the attempt. "The hell are you *doing?*" I demand.

"Defend yourself. Trust in your weapon and your ability. Don't *fight* with yourself. Let go--it will come naturally," Shields tells me.

I am so pissed that I do so and immediately feel the sword become an extension of my hand. Before I know it, I have bested Shields and am standing over him as he signals defeat. Out of breath and surprised, he slapped the sword away and gets up.

"Well done! Your Origin would be proud."

"Who *is* my Origin?" I ask. I have been trying for the longest to get him to answer that question.

"You are the Echo of Spartacus," Shields reveals.

"For *real?*" I didn't know what to make of it.

"How much do you actually *know* about Spartacus?"

Shields asked.

Other than the fact that I'd loved Andy Whitfield and never missed an episode of *Spartacus* on Starz, I didn't know much at all about him.

I know he was one of the greatest warriors who ever lived.

"A bit--the basics really, and what I've seen on TV."

"Spartacus was a Thracian. Thrace encompassed what today includes Greece, Bulgaria, and Turkey. On a mission to conquer the world and expand the Empire, the Romans took Thrace and Spartacus, sentencing him to slavery. Lentulus Batiatus purchased Spartacus and brought him to his gladiator school outside Capua, in what is now southern Italy. While enslaved, Spartacus met Crixus and Oenomaus, two gladiators who were also owned by Batiatus and would later become his seconds in command." Shields nods thoughtfully.

"In 73 B.C., Spartacus led a revolt with Crixus and Oenomaus, they threw off their chains, and started the Third Servile War. Gathering strength and size as an army, he freed slaves and led them into battle against the Romans. The slave army grew to upwards of 70,000 men and won several encounters against Legatus Claudius Glaber before the Romans began to take them seriously.

"Running out of options, Rome looked for a solution and found it in Marcus Licinius Crassus -- a name you should be familiar with by now. Crassus was the wealthiest man in the empire and offered his services to destroy Spartacus and his slave militia. After failing to reach a truce with Crassus, Spartacus's soldiers were slaughtered. Those who survived the ordeal were crucified and placed on display to be made examples of."

"What happened to Spartacus?" I ask.

"His body was never found. People said that he perished in that final battle, but he made it out alive. He searched for and found his wife, who had also been captured and sold into slavery by the Romans. He freed her, and they lived out the rest of their days as farmers in the outer regions of Greece."

The story inspired me. With my first fight coming up in two weeks, I finally feel ready. I have been waiting for two years to step back into a ring.

"The first event of the year is only two weeks away," he went on. "This is what you've been waiting for. You're getting the chance to test your skill against an opponent who wants your blood. I have something for you, a gift. Come with me to my office. You'll want to see this."

What could it be? The suspense is almost paralyzing. Upon entering the office, Shields says, "Close the door," and turns to the bookcase on the wall adjacent to his desk.

Sitting on the second to last shelf was a black trinket box with ancient-looking figural decoration. Shields removes an old key from a small chest and slid a few books to the side, revealing a keyhole. He inserts the key and pulls back the entire bookcase, which is actually a door.

"This way," he says.

I follow him through the portal and peer down a darkened staircase illuminated by torches positioned high on the stone walls. At the bottom, it opens onto a long passage that runs at least twenty yards.

At the other end, Shields turns to confirm I am still following him before he ventures further down the hidden passage. I start to feel on edge, preparing myself for anything we might find.

When I catch up with him, he says, "We're here. This room houses legendary weapons collected over the centuries by previous Aurelius members. Only members of this house are privy to what's in here. Welcome to the Arsenal."

He pushes open a massive wooden door. Inside I find a marble storeroom containing an extensive collection of weapons. Fluorescent lights, air filtration, and a temperature control system were built to maintain the items in the room. There are racks, shelves, and tables full of arms. Twelve columns supported the ceiling, divided into 4 rows, three columns per row. In between each column, glass cases showcase the most notable weapons.

At the end of the room, on the wall, hangs a massive gold letter--twenty feet high and ten feet across at the base--that resembles an "A." Just beneath it, two swords lay on a podium.

"Where is this place?" I ask.

"We're under the training room. This is the mark of Aurelius--and these swords are yours."

"Whoa! These are intense. . . Not to sound ungrateful or anything, but why are you giving them to *me?*"

He silences the irreverent tone in my voice with a level stare, and I purse my lips and raise my eyebrows. "They are the *Falcata*, the personal weapons, of Alexander the Great. He conquered the world with these swords. Upon his death, the blades disappeared for centuries but, in time, reemerged in possession of the Roman emperor Numerian, whose short reign ended in 284 AD, as a spoil of war. Numerian had the original Arsenal built to house the weapons of conquered kings. But, since he held joint reign with his older brother, he felt he needed to find a way to separate himself as his own entity.

Numerian was commended for his creation--but raised suspicion for his work's secrecy, and Numerian was perceived as a spy. As a result, the Senate, utterly unaware of Legacy, had him assassinated. However, those who knew about Legacy continued the contest and, realizing the economic potential of the wagers associated with it, agreed that Legacy would need to expand."

Shields sank onto a wooden stool in an alcove of the room and motioned to me to join him. One of the torches is casting fleeting shadows across the side of his face; the light seemed to make his eyes glow.

Shields goes on, "the original members sent word to trusted men of means and the officials of surrounding lands. As a result, forces were joined, and four initial sects were created to establish identity among the parties. The senators who created this Sect chose to name the entity Aurelius in honor of Rome's last great emperor. They lived by the motto *beati sumus deorum*--"blessed are we by the gods." The senators protected the Arsenal and gave their best fighters the most extraordinary weapons they had. The tradition has continued ever since."

These identical swords have blades twenty inches long, two and a half wide, and are smithed out of steel. During Alexander's time, the Greeks had made theirs out of copper. So someone must have recast the blades to make them stronger. The swords weigh about five pounds each and are as sharp as surgical scalpels. The cross-guards are made of gold, with a pearl handle grip. The grips are curved towards the ends and have individual finger molds for better gripping.

There are lions' heads on the pommels to represent the ferocity with which Alexander fought.

"There are great fighters in Aurelius," Shields says, breaking the momentary silence, "but you have the potential to be the best. Train hard, fighter harder, and you will reap reward greater than you can possibly dream."

He leaves the Arsenal while I am still in there just staring at the swords. I walk to the center of the room to get acquainted with the weapons-- I begin shadow fighting, imagining I am in the arena, counter-moving, attacking, and blocking my opponent's attacks. I am so focused I start to feel Spartacus coming through my arms.

Suddenly, I am in the arena as Spartacus, battling a man twice his size. This memory--it *feels* like a memory--is so vivid before long that I am consciously making all his moves. It ends when I deal the final blow and drive my sword through the man's heart. The crowd cheers ardently, chanting Spartacus in waves of sound that swept around the arena.

Leaving the Arsenal, I don't know what to do with myself. I am full of life and energy. I rush back to the apartment with the swords in my bag. McKenna isn't home yet, and I thought I would do something nice for her.

Her favorite food is shrimp Alfredo, so I decide to go out and buy the ingredients so I can make dinner.

A few hours later, I hear her keys jingling in the door. When she opens it, I tell her to wait for a second and that I have a surprise. I cover her eyes and navigate her to the kitchen.

"Something smells good," she says.

"I had a good day today, so I figured that I could do something to make yours better, too."

"What did you do?" McKenna asks, with a skeptical tone in her voice.

"I had to do something wrong? Can't I just do nice

things for you because I want to?"

"Okay... Do you know what next week is?"

"Our third anniversary! Did you think I'd forget?"

"I did, honestly."

We discuss plans for our anniversary over dinner. We decide to go out to eat and then to another party being thrown by Aurelius.

When we finish our meal, we head to the living room for a while. I figure it is the perfect time to talk about Legacy. I know discretion is the primary injunction, but how would I explain myself if I get cut in a fight, or even worse? She wouldn't know what to do with herself if something happens to me.

"I need to tell you something," I position.

McKenna shifts her focus so she can intently hear what I am going to say.

"I'm fighting again. And, I have a fight coming up soon."

"Okay. I know you're happy about that."

"Aurelius isn't a fraternity," I began. "Not the way you think it is. It's, uh, it's part of a bigger institution known as Legacy. It's an entire world of modern-day warriors known as Bloodborns, who fight in the manner of the people they descend from, with real weapons, and I don't want to go into the fight without you knowing."

"Wait. *What?* . . . You're serious, aren't you?"

"Yeah. I had to tell you because I don't want you to get concerned if I came home one night battered and bleeding. There is always a possibility of being hurt when I'm fighting, but more so now."

She leaned back against the sofa cushions and stared for a moment at the ceiling. "I trust your judgment," she says after a long pause, "and know that if you were unsure of yourself or this, Legacy, you wouldn't even be entertaining it, so I'm okay with it. But I'm coming to every single one of your fights, and that is non-negotiable."

I'm not surprised she wanted to come. I'd probably have been shocked if she hadn't. I wasn't too sure how I would get her in, but I'd figure something out. If I have to pay her way there, I would.

"So, explain to me what exactly a Bloodborn is?" she says.

"Bloodborns are the descendants of the greatest known warriors throughout the ages. Legacy has been around since the latter years of the Roman Empire. There are these people called, Historians who research and follow bloodlines. They can predict in what generation a person whose blood has ties to one of history's elite will manifest Bloodborn ability. I'm told that Legacy very rarely comes across a Bloodborn of my--well, my caliber. I'm what they call an Echo. An Echo is a doppelganger of their Origin."

"Doppelganger--like a double? Who is your Origin?"

"I am, it seems, the Echo of Spartacus," I reveal.

"Well, Mr. Spartacus, I'll be in the crowd watching you become a legend once again."

I feel a weight lift off my shoulders when I finish telling her. It wasn't that big of a secret, but it's something that I needed to say.

After class the next day, I went to the house to train as usual. Most days, Linc and I pair up. My training has been going well; I'm already considered one of the best fighters in Aurelius, along with Nikko and Linc. Though I hadn't had a fight in Legacy, I was just more experienced than most of the house members.

Linc is very skilled. He uses a sword and a shield, the latter as protection and valuable in battle, though I didn't want one. I am more offensive. I used two swords so I can deflect and attack quicker. We train for about two hours before calling it a day. Linc asked about McKenna and tells me how Juliet is.

"We had a good time with you guys at the party," I tell him.

"Yeah. Us, too. Decent party," Linc says, "I don't know how Owen got in, but he was lucky Nikko broke it up. Nikko is all about honor. After all, he is a Relic."

"Was Juliet okay? Those guys didn't hurt her or anything, did they?"

"Jules was okay. She's a firecracker--oh, and that reminds me. I never thanked you for stepping in when you did. I'm glad you could see what was happening because I had no idea."

"Hey, McKenna was there, too. I would never allow anything to happen to them. . . Who, by the way, is your Origin?" I had never asked before and am curious.

" Syphax. Maybe you've heard of him. He was king of the ancient tribe of the Masaesyli in western Numidia. In 213 BC, he allied himself with the Romans and went to war against the Massylians of eastern Numidia. The assault was successful, and Syphax gained territory in eastern Numidia. He died in 203 BC, after being delivered to Scipio Africanus as a prisoner."

I think that's remarkable. How could something so elaborate still exist and be a thriving institution? I've always been a person who would jump at the chance to learn something new. The history in Legacy is like a time machine to the people who had laid the foundation for today's world. We tend to take for granted where we came from; if you were to search your bloodlines, where would they take you? Would you even have the balls to find out? There is no future without a past, and we can't figure out where we're going unless we know where we came from.

When we finish up for the day, I head through the campus on my way back to the apartment. I hear someone yelling my name and turn to see Nikko heading toward me. Since the incident at Haze, we had become pretty good friends.

"What's up, dude?" he asks.

"Nothing much. Where you off to?"

"I've got to go handle some family business. Are you ready for your first Proelium?"

"Think so. I've been waiting a long time to get back into action. I want the day to be here already."

"That's good. Just make sure to prep yourself."

"Prep for what?" I don't know what he was referring to. Was this not just going to be a fight like any other?

"When you're fighting in the arena, taking a hit isn't the same as when you're in the cage. Receiving a blow from a razor-sharp weapon is more painful than you can imagine. If and when you do get cut, just keep moving. Your adrenaline will keep the pain under wraps for the remainder of the match. After that, though, it's another story."

I had almost forgotten about that possibility. I am so used to barely being touched when I fought in the cage. Every weapon is made as sharp as possible and maintained that way. You can drop an apple from a foot away, and these blades will slice right through it. Just thinking about that is making me cringe. I quickly change the subject.

"So, if you don't mind me asking, you're a Relic, right?"

"Yeah, I am."

"What exactly is that?"

"Relics are Bloodborns whose families still practice the same traditions as their Origins. My family has been aware of and participated in Legacy for centuries. You could even say we are an institution. Because of this long-standing tradition of battle success, we've maintained the custom of praying to the same gods as our Origins. Why not? It's kept us alive this long."

"How did your ancestors know about Legacy?" I ask.

"When Troy was burned down, Andromache, the wife of Hector, was going to start over but didn't get far before the Greeks were once again on their tails. Fearing death for herself and her son, she had her most beloved maid take Astyanax away while she stayed behind to slow the Greek advance. Hector had valuables stowed away for his wife and son so they could continue to live well in the case of his death-- sort of a life insurance policy.

Eventually, the Greeks started to gain on them. Andromache left the location of the valuables with her son and sacrificed herself to give the maid and Astyanax a chance to escape. He never used his inheritance, but he kept a close watch over it, passing it down through generations.

When Legacy was created, my ancestor Agapetus, a Bloodborn himself, was approached by one of the original founding senators he happened to know. Recognizing his great skill as a warrior, that senator made him an offer. From that day on, when a child of my family is a Bloodborn, we take our place as Aurelius legacies."

"Hector would be proud."

"I too believe he would be. The thing that made Hector, a phenomenal warrior was not the fact that he was exceptionally skilled. He loved his country and his people. He fought, not for glory or honor, but for his people to continue their peaceful lives. He was a devoted husband, father, and a warrior last."

Real men, Nikko was saying, are respectable people who carry themselves in a manner that befits a gentleman. That's how I try to be for McKenna.

I am relieved to be home. Training has been exhausting. I find McKenna sitting, watching TV on the couch, so I join her. Going to parties and on dates is nice, but McKenna and I got most of our enjoyment from just sitting on the couch together. We love throwing on sweats, cuddling up with a bowl of popcorn, and watching movies and a long list of our favorite TV shows. We flip through the channel guide, searching for something to watch, and finally settled on a show we both love. A marathon of the series is playing on the network; we watch every second until we fall asleep on the couch.

When I wake up the next day, McKenna has already left. There is a note on the coffee table for me: *Good morning, stud. You were so cute sleeping like a little princess that I didn't want to disturb you.*

I made you breakfast—it's your favorite, Fruity Pebbles. The box is sitting on the table—and a bowl and spoon with your name on them. Text me when you wake up. Love you, xoxo.

Still tired, I get myself off the couch and try to get it together. I take a shower, eat breakfast, and head over to Aurelius. With the Proelium coming up, I still have a lot of work to prepare for my first fight. With weapons in hand, it is time for me to get my body armor fitted. I went to the equipment room and met the equipment handler, a nice old man named Doc, a little quirky, but he knows his stuff.

When it came to the equipment, he's a bit of a mad scientist. Doc fashions armor that's adapted the original look of the pieces to modern expression. When I shake his hand, it is rough, and he has a noticeably raspy voice; I can tell he is a true craftsman.

"So, what kind of armor do you have for me?" I ask.

"I've created something special for you, Mr. Hart. In Legacy, it is customary for fighters to want to immortalize their Origins. They dress and wear armor that is in some respects traditional to their Origin and cultural customs. I don't expect you to sport the brief that past gladiators wore, but there are a few things you do need. Greaves, Cuirass, Bracers and a Helmet."

"No helmet--I don't want to wear one." I know it would be wise to, but I feel it's distracting. When I fight, I need to make eye contact with my opponent. I want him to be able to see the focus and determination in my eyes. Fighting me is like standing face to face with a wild beast; if you make a wrong move, you may meet your end."

"All right--your choice, everything but a Helmet. Shall I explain the function of these items?"

"Yeah, I would like to know," I say.

"Right. Well, your greaves are the pieces of armor that protect your shins. They consist of a rigid material and padding to absorb direct strikes. They can also work well in delivering hard blows to your opponents. Your Bracers will protect your forearms. The Cuirass might be your most important piece of armor. This chest plate protects your torso from being turned into Swiss cheese. Without it, you're more vulnerable to blade wounds, being stabbed in a vital organ, or being killed. Typically, steel would be the metal of choice for these, but I have developed a titanium alloy that is nearly weightless and almost indestructible.

Like the original Cuirasses, yours resembles a bare torso. The pecs, abs, and obliques are defined on the plate, allowing for easy maneuverability. I've also added decorative moldings of lions to both pecs to resemble the handles of your swords. The metal, as you can see, is painted a matte black, the moldings gray."

These things are sick. I am impressed. Doc brought up a good point, too, that I hadn't thought of until he made reference to it. What am I going to wear? When I fought in the cage, I only wore thigh-length shorts in addition to my gloves. This is different. I won't look right in shorts and armor.

I don't stay long for my training session today. It is our anniversary, and McKenna and I have plans to celebrate. We rendezvoused at the apartment. She is already getting prepared when I get home. McKenna had just got out of the shower and is doing her hair and makeup. I don't need much time to get ready, so I hop in the shower before getting dressed.

"What are you going to wear tonight?" she asks.

"I don't know yet--I was just going to throw on something nice."

"Throw on something nice? It's our *anniversary!* You don't just throw something on nice. I bought you something to wear-- it's on the bed."

I have simple tastes in clothing. I've never much cared about what I wore, though I hardly looked like a slob, always wearing dark colors, fitted tees, and slim-fit jeans. McKenna, on the other hand, is very stylish. She takes pride in the clothes she wears, always dressing appropriately for any occasion.

"Clothes are the first impression you give people," she says. I didn't mind that she'd bought something for me to wear; it was thoughtful, and I'm sure she knew exactly what I would like.

I turn off the water, grab my towel, and dry off. McKenna is in the bedroom when I enter to find a bag on my side of the bed. When I open it, I am not disappointed by the long-sleeved knit top, new jeans, and black boots.

"Well? What do you think?" she asks.

I put on the clothes and look in the mirror to see how they fit. They are perfect. I start smiling and turn to her.

"You don't have to say anything. I can tell by the look on your face that I know what I am doing. You're welcome!" McKenna says as she enters the closet and pulls out another bag of clothes.

"You bought a new outfit?"

"Hello, it's our *anniversary!* I want to look special. Besides, you don't think I would buy you a new outfit and not get something for myself, do you? I'll be ready in ten minutes."

While I wait for her, I turn on the TV. She'd said ten minutes, but there were days when waiting for her to get ready; ten minutes could turn into thirty in no time. Luckily, today isn't one of them; in no time, she appears in the doorway.

"Ready?" she asks.

I peer at the door as she stands there in the new little black number. The race-back tank dress had an iridescent overlay that gave it an eye-catching shimmer. Black pumps highlighted her long statuesque legs.

"Stunning!" I say. There is no other way to say it.

We make our way to dinner. I have made reservations for us at Soleil, a charming French restaurant spoken very highly of, with a laid-back, pleasant ambiance, efficient and polite service, and food to die for.

The cozy table they sat us at, nestled in the heart of Soleil, is the perfect setting, dinnerware placed with precision, white tablecloth hugging our thighs. A low glass container with a red phalaenopsis, anchored in place by submerged river stones, sits in the middle of the table, with a tea candle that seems to float weightlessly on the surface.

"This is beautiful," McKenna says.

"A toast to us," I say when the wine comes, a chilled bottle of *sauvignon blanc.* "On this day three years ago, we professed our commitment to one another, though it feels like our fire was forged in a life time before we even met. I will love you across any plain, unconditionally till my last breath."

She gazes at me. Fighting to hold back tears, she mouths those three words, *I love you.*

Dinner is perfect, a smooth transition from appetizers to entrees. We decide to forego the movies-- the food had been so filling and delicious it left us a bit tired. All we want to do was go home and lie in each other's arms.

The Proelium is days away, and I am more ready than ever. I have been chomping at the bit to enter the arena after living through the recollections of Spartacus. I want to feel the sensation that comes from standing before an audience of five thousand screaming fans chanting my name. Bobby and I sit in Shields' class, waiting for the period to end.

When it does, Shields tells us to stay.

"Have a nice rest, Bobby?" He asks as Bobby wipes the drool from his cheek. "This won't take long. With the Proelium coming up, I need you to be ready, Luke. The Assembly members have chosen your opponent, and they haven't gone easy on you. Because of your experience and the fact that you're an Echo, they want to see exactly what you're capable of."

"What's the Assembly?" I ask.

"Bobby will discuss that with you later. Right now, I need you two to pay attention. Your opponent for the Proelium is Baldr, the Bloodborn of Erik The Red. This guy is not to be taken lightly. He's a brute and doesn't go down easily. If you're not ready, you may find yourself in a world of hurt. Bobby, brief Luke on Baldr--I have a meeting I must get to."

Shields leaves in a hurry.

"I wonder where *he's* going," I say but turn my attention to the trainee. Bobby, I know, was going to be a great Historian. "So? What can you tell me about Baldr?"

"Well, first off, he is without question the Bloodborn of a Viking. If you Google-imaged Modern *Viking*, you will find a picture of the guy. He's a mountain, easily upwards of 300 pounds, long hair, and he has a neck as thick as your thigh. I once saw him take a spear to the shoulder, and that didn't even phase him. He pulled out the spear-like it was a splinter, wiped his fingers in the blood, and tasted it before he demolished his opponent. 'Tough' doesn't begin to describe him."

I'm not worried; he isn't the biggest guy I had ever fought. I will fight him just as I would everyone else-- let the match come to me and react when I have an opening. If that doesn't work, then it will have to be a brawl. Either way, Baldr is nothing more than my next fall guy.

But the Proelium is two days away, and it is time for me to live up to the name.

"Thanks, that's all I need to know. You hungry?"

We haven't hung out in a while. I have time to kill, and I want to see what Bobby has been up to. We go to a diner so I can grab a burger. I know a lot about Bobby's family history but have no idea of his personal life.

"So, what's up, Bro? How have you been?" I ask.

"Not bad, man, just working as usual."

"I know what you mean. McKenna and I have been dog-tired lately. Most nights, we end up falling asleep in front of the TV."

"That's not a bad thing, you know. I wish I had someone to fall asleep on the couch with."

"Isn't there anyone?" I ask.

"I've had girlfriends before, but you know how that goes. Nothing works out; there's no trust. You're not what they want right now. I don't know. There is one girl I've had my eye on from my physics class, Kanae. It's Japanese, and it means 'beautiful one.' She's real pretty--that classical sort of beautiful. We've talked a bit in class, but she would never go for a guy like me."

"I wouldn't be so sure if I were you," I say. "Next time you talk to Kanae, pay attention to her body language and what she says. If she has a warm, open body gesture towards you, you have half the battle won. Talk to her about something other than class. Try to make the conversation about *her*. If she's engaged and wants to keep talking, then you're in. No woman talks to a guy they don't like. Trust me, you'll know--there is *always* a chance."

We stay a while longer. Eventually, we part ways, and I head home. All I am focused on is the Proelium.

For the next two days, all I do is eat, sleep, and train.

I am ready to fight, and everyone is going to find out just how much.

There is one thing I take heed of. McKenna tells me about a dream she had the night before that had scared her because of how vivid it was. According to her, the vision was so relevant, it felt like a prophecy.

"You went to battle and were killed," she says. "You saw your opponent as just another unassuming person. He was as strong as an ox, and he took your life. Luke, *please* be careful tonight." She knows about the Proelium and, in fact, is going to come—there's no way I can fight without her there. She would never forgive herself if I got hurt and she wasn't with me.

"Wait for a second," she adds. McKenna gets out of bed and hurries to the closet. There is a red dress hanging from the door. She grabs it and tears a swatch off the bottom. "Here, I want you to take this." She says, handing me the swatch. "Wear it around your hand, so you remember what I said."

I meet Shields and the other members of Aurelius at the house. Linc, Taylor, and Nikko are also fighting in the Proelium. Taylor is the Bloodborn of King

Arthur's most trusted knight, Lancelot. Taylor will be the first of us to enter the arena tonight. Followed by Linc, me, and finally Nikko.

We are embraced by our brothers and wished good luck before we leave for the event. We travel to the arena as a single unit. The others will be watching from the stands and cheering us on. McKenna and Juliet are coming with Bobby. He and I figured that if they go with him, he can say that they too work for Aurelius, so there shouldn't be any problem getting them in.

McKenna told me that Juliet has never been to a fight even though she was aware of Legacy--she's been too afraid that something will happen to Linc. Though, since McKenna is coming, she is willing to go for the first time.

We reach the site, a building called, The Sphere, named after the glass dome, made up of individual triangular sections that encase the entire arena, an impressive architectural feat.

To maintain privacy, Legacy has private armed security constantly patrolling the grounds. Local police have been prohibited by higher powers from coming near the area. I ask Shields why the guards aren't carrying guns.

"They're forbidden from entering the world of Legacy," he tells me. "There's no honor in a gun. It's a coward's weapon of choice. If you want to take a man's life, do it up close with your own hands."

The Sphere is on the wharf, only a couple of miles from our headquarters. I've never been inside but was under the impression that it was a performing arts center. I guess it moonlighted as a theatre of war.

The stage is set; the smell of the harbor fills the parking lot as we make our way past thousands of cars parked outside. You can tell from the retail value of some of them that whatever gala was going on inside requires a great deal of money.

Instead of entering through a back entrance, fighters are made to parade through the crowd--the Legacy fanatics want to assess the men they would be betting their money on up close.

It is almost as if we are thoroughbreds at the Kentucky derby.

The main hallway circles the arena walls. The massive building has black marble floors, arched doorways, and torches burning high on tall Greek columns. Towering statues of history's greatest warriors stand as proud memorials to those men and women who had forged the world of Legacy.

Like the Coliseum in Rome, the Flavian Amphitheatre. The sand-covered floor of the Sphere is arranged in the shape of a bowl. Seating rose above the pitch and was filled with blood-crazed patrons eagerly waiting for the first contest.

The locker rooms lay beneath the arena floor--the arena pitch is operated entirely from the hypogeum. Shields walks us to our quarters, where we suit up for battle. Doc had sent our weapons ahead of our arrival. He maintains them at an optimal state of readiness for combat.

Each one of my Aurelius brothers has a pre-game ritual. Taylor is in the hall, practicing his handiwork with the sword. Linc is working out in the corner, doing push-ups, pull-ups, and dips to warm his body and make himself ready to fight. Nikko's pre-game is something I'd never seen before. I didn't grasp the true meaning of Relic until I saw him praying for victory to the god Apollo.

Different, to say the least, but I can't concern myself with that. I have no pre-game ritual, just focus. I fastened on my armor and visualize myself destroying Baldr. For me fighting is like chess. I can see the game several moves ahead. This intuition allows me to play out the match in my head before I ever touch the floor.

My Everlast hand wraps are perfectly secure. Greaves, bracers, and cuirass firmly fixed to my chest, forearms, and legs.

I am wearing black combat boots and pants. I tie the strip of red material McKenna had given me around my right hand and wrist. My two *falcata* are sharpened and ready to spill blood.

Shields enters the room to give us a pep talk. "I wanted to talk to you before you take to the sand. This is the first Proelium of the year. Fight with courage and honor, and you will bring glory to our house.

For the Brotherhood!"

"For Aurelius!" we shout in return.

We leave the barracks and head to the arena. Standing behind a massive fifteen-foot gate, we wait for Taylor to be called in.

Shields pulls me aside.

"It's showtime. Are you ready?"

"I was born ready."

"Good. Then go out there and give these people what they came for, blood. Whenever you fight, mercy must not exist! If they step in the arena with you, there's only one option. Win if you want to live, do whatever it takes to survive! Pour a man's blood on the sand, and you will be rewarded with all the glory and treasures that come in this life. Remember, death is only a casualty of victory!"

I think about that and the dream McKenna had and know there is no way I won't be ready for Baldr. Taylor and Linc both win their fights. That must have been great for Juliet to see--it should give her more confidence in Linc as a fighter and that he will not get hurt.

And then my time came.

I close my eyes and just listen for my name to be called. Whatever is going on in the world is irrelevant. All that matters is being present in this moment.

The crowd falls silent and focuses their attention on the solarium as the Master of Ceremonies begins to speak. "Tonight, we give you carnage in its most imposing form--the giant Baldr of Valhalla, Bloodborn of Viking King, Eric the Red."

The crowd roars as the gate on the opposite end of the arena rose, and Baldr saunters out. He throws up his arms and shouts something in Nordic. I have no idea what he says, but the Valhalla fans applaud. Their support makes no difference. As soon as my gate lifts, he is going to have to defend himself.

"Prayers," the announcer went on, "have as well been answered tonight in the form of a true hero. At long last, the greatest gladiator, and arguably the greatest warrior of all time, has returned--Spartacus! True reward indeed. For only the fourth time in recent Legacy history, has an Echo appeared on the sand. It is my privilege to give you Luke of Aurelius, the Echo of Spartacus, God of the Arena!"

The gate opens, and I emerge from the shadows of the dark corridor. Time lingers as I enter the light; the calm pounding of my heartbeat is the only thing I hear. The crowd stands to their feet and explodes in ovation; I can feel the radiant energy of their anticipation. I grip my swords and face Baldr in the center of the arena. He has a shield in his right arm and a war hammer in the other. A loud percussion from the beating of his guard hits my chest to intimidate me.

The Master of Ceremonies initiates the fight, and there is no turning back now. Baldr and I lock eyes and, without hesitation, rush towards one another.

He swung his mighty hammer as if he intended to knock me out with one blow. I duck, rolling out of the way. He is surprisingly quick, considering how hefty he is. I keep that in mind as I advance forward.

He uses his shield to block my attack with the right sword and his hammer to deflect the left. I'm not going to win the fight anytime soon if I continue to hold these weapons. The match goes on the same way for another minute; both of our attacks effectively parried. I am outraged when he lands one good blow to my chin with his shield. I manage to avoid his next thrust and found my opening in time to deliver a knee-weakening blow with my sword to his back. The strike opens him up from one shoulder blade to the other. His arms drop, and I lunge at him and driving my knee into his left temple. He falls backward, hitting the ground like a tree. In an instance, I mount his chest, using my left arm to secure him to the floor while I pounded his face into a gory pulp.

With one last monumental effort, he lifts his arm, extending his index and middle fingers to concede. Somewhere through my anger, I find it in me to stop raining blows on his face. I stand and face my audience as they pass judgment on what they just witnessed. As soon as I look at the sea of faces, cheers and praise rain down as they honor me. I raise my fist to the crowd in respect and recognition.

I can bask in this feeling forever.

CHAPTER 4: SOMETHING IS WRONG!

The first Proelium went well--Aurelius swept the event from Valhalla. Nikko fought with honor and secured the win, though Nikko hadn't much excitement in the arena. He doesn't take risks; he just relies on his solid nature and skill. That's why he's never lost a fight. He fights for his family; for Aurelius, he fights to win.

Afterward, Nikko hosted another party at Haze in celebration of our victory. There were no party crashers this time, only Aurelius fighters and affiliates. It was a great way to cap off the night.

I take the next day off, figuring I should rest but

that I'll be back in the gym tomorrow. McKenna heads out with Juliet so that they can have a girl's day.

"I'll be back in few hours--we're just going shopping," she tells me.

"Okay. I have to go by the House. Shields wants to talk to me."

"What about?"

"I don't know."

"Well, I'm off. I'm taking the car. Try not to miss me too much!"

On my way to Aurelius, images of the Proelium keep replaying in my head. It was by far the most exciting fight I've ever been in. Baldr was a good fighter, one of the best I've faced. Had I not listened to Shields and McKenna, I would probably have gone into the fight thinking nothing of my opponent's skill.

When I arrive, Shields had left the door open, so I knock and glance in. Shields is behind his desk, and a man is sitting across from him.

"Luke, come in," Shields calls out. I can't see the man's face, only dark pants and polished shoes.

"I'd like to introduce you to Thomas Goodwin."

Goodwin rose from his seat and extends his hand to me.

"It's a pleasure to finally meet the new bad boy of Legacy in person. A great fight last night--your Origin would've been proud." He is middle-aged and has a full head of graying brown hair and an even grayer beard. I can tell from the camaraderie between them that the two are old friends. There is something familiar about Thomas; I can't quite figure it out.

"Thank you, sir; nice to meet you as well. If you don't mind me asking, how do you and Professor Shields know each other?"

"Oh, we've been friends for many years. How long now?" he asks, turning to Shields.

"Twenty years."

"Twenty years, that's it. The good professor and I met when he first joined Aurelius. Even then, he was a great fighter, the Echo of the Lionhearted. He still fights that way." Goodwin paused before adding, "I believe you and my son have become good friends?"

"I'm sorry, I don't believe I--"

"Shields hasn't told you much about me, I see. I'm

the Historian. Bobby is my son and apprentice. I've been tracking you since you were born. You're the second Echo I've found since I took over the work. Shields was the first."

Then I remembered where I'd seen him before, on numerous occasions. I'd always thought they were coincidences. He'd been following me. He'd also been in the crowd that fateful night in Rome.

We spoke for a while about Legacy, Spartacus, and the other Echoes in Legacy. Just weeks before, Shields had mentioned in passing that other Echoes were out there but had never gone into detail.

Goodwin talks about the other Houses and how the Proelium works. "By now, you should be familiar with at least three Houses in Legacy, as my son tells it. You've already become acquainted with a few members of the House of Crassus. He told me you and Owen were just moments away from facing off with one another. I would've paid money to see you annihilate him."

"Back to what I was saying, though. There are eight sects of Legacy, five of which are in the U.S.--Aurelius,

Crassus, Valhalla, Khan, and Ares. There are only four Echoes known to Legacy. You, the Echo of Spartacus. Shields, the Echo of King Richard. Kenji, the Echo of Miyamoto Musashi. And Owen, the Echo of Achilles.

You don't need to worry about the other three sects right now. You only would face them if specially asked to by the Assembly. The Proelium is held four times a year. The final Proelium is like the Superbowl of Legacy. Only then can you be summoned to battle any fighter. Usually, the best gladiators are brought together to face each other in the final Proelium of the year."

This is all new information to me. I've only gotten bits and pieces of information about this world since I've been here. No wonder Shields and Goodwin are great friends.

There is a question I want to ask Goodwin that's been on my mind. Before the first Proelium, Shields had mentioned the Assembly, and the name had just come up again. Shields had told me to ask Bobby about the Assembly, but I never got around to doing so. This, I thought, is a perfect time.

"What is the Assembly?" I ask.

"The council of Legacy. The committee was formed to enforce the laws of Legacy. Six warriors who had long since touched the sand of the arena were entrusted with the responsibility. Five rules were put into place to protect warriors during competition, and they're strictly implemented.

"Rule #1: Warriors could not be slaves. Everyone who fights in Legacy is a free man, with the free will to choose his or her own fate. And every fighter must be compensated for any victory in Legacy.

Rule #2: Fighters are free to join any sect they please. But while a sect member, a fighter cannot be approached by a controlling member of an opposing party. They must not be influenced into new membership.

Rule #3: At no time is a member of another sect allowed to set foot on the opposing House's territory.

Rule #4: Only approved individuals are granted to be in the audience of Legacy. People of substantial means are available to purchase arena seating. Discretion is of the utmost value. If any person is caught exposing the world of Legacy, the consequence is punishable by death.

Rule #5: Every fighter is to be granted a fair fight. Every gladiator has the right to a warrior's death."

These ideas sink into me as the complete picture of this world is revealed. This institution was created to last, like all things in ancient Rome. So many have known about Legacy, though most don't. If they did, they'd realize that Numerian was just as influential as the man he shared his name with.

"These rules were initially different, and eventually, the idea of individually controlled sects faded out. Once that happened, the Assembly assumed complete control over Legacy. When this power shift occurred, more and more rules and regulations started to appear. Before long, the Assembly was controlling everything--even who would be fighting in the bouts.

"The new Legacy institution outraged those who still supported the individual sects. The way they saw it, the Assembly had become a corrupt band of tyrants. The Assembly began manufacturing fights for profit, even going as far as ordering the deaths of several fighters who begged for mercy. . .

There was only one way to end that control. The supporters of individual sects gathered a band of warriors to march on the Assembly and kill them all. They called themselves Shade, and they operated in total secrecy. It is believed that the group wore black-hooded cloaks as a way of remaining unrecognizable. But their effort was unsuccessful. To safeguard themselves, the Assembly autocrats began to control Legacy from behind closed doors, and Shade found refuge in the shadows."

"Are these plans to overthrow the Assembly still in the works?" I ask.

"Personally, I still support the idea of sects being controlled individually. As long as the Assembly is still around, it will continue to hold power. As far as Shade, they were never heard from again. Some say the faction is still around, waiting for the perfect moment to strike. It's generally agreed among the Historians, though, that Shade died off shortly after it was first formed." Goodwin explains.

"Telling ghost stories, are we, Thomas?" a voice asks from the doorway. I look at Shields' face; he has a fiery look in his eye. When I turned to see, the man I saw had a dark presence about him, or maybe it was the pompous tone exuding from him that made me think so. Goodwin and Shields' body language changes dramatically.

"What are you doing here?" Shields demanded.

"There's no need to be so tense, Shieldsie. I've simply come to meet the marvelous new Legacy gladiator I've heard so much about. Is this he, the Echo of Spartacus?" The man asks. "How are you doing, son. My name is Lazarus Caius Crassus. I hear you're quite an Echo. A pleasure to meet the Decimator of Baldr."

"The gratification is not mutual," I instinctively reply.

"Oh, wonderful! Such tenacity. You really do embody him. Thomas, you've outdone yourself this time. What a find! You'd have done well to join with Crassus," he dryly adds as he turns to examine me.

His arrogance is stunning, and I wonder why he has come. Shields is throwing daggers at Crassus with his eyes.

"You have no business here, Lazarus," he says in a flat, brittle voice. "Whatever thought conjured you here has left you dangerously out of your element. You would do well to leave immediately--or be escorted out."

"All right, Shieldsie--no need to be so crude. I'll leave. Thomas, it was a pleasure as always. Luke, I wish you the best. We will see each other again shortly." He bows his head in a gesture of promise. The image of those dark eyes leaves an eerie imprint in my mind. Shields watches every step as Crassus heads out of the building. I can tell the man is bad news.

"I take it he is the head of Crassus?" I ask.

Shields is infuriated. "Lazarus Caius Crassus is the most detestable man alive. He's a dark horse, along with that entire house. He has a thirst for blood and reaching a higher position. He purchases mercenaries, not fighters--Legacy is more about history and sport than bereavement."

"Crassus is not and never was a fighter," Goodwin says. "His family has bought its way through history. Marcus Licinius Crassus was the wealthiest man in Rome. When Claudius Glaber failed to destroy the slave army led by Spartacus, Rome appointed Crassus to assume military command and move against him. Hungry for more than a political position, Crassus was the only person willing to do the job.

"In 71 BC, at the Battle of Silver River, Crassus defeated the slave army. It was believed that Spartacus had fallen in that battle. Obviously, the belief was false. And Crassus's only connection to being a soldier is unsuccessfully destroying the slave leader. That's why he was so eager to meet you. Crassus's history only exists through name and money now because Marcus Crassus failed his mission. Spartacus lived then and still lives now through you.

"Being the wealthiest man in Rome made it easy for Crassus to assure the longevity of his name. In 284 AD, when Numerian and the Senators started Legacy, Gnaeus Crassus, the descendant of Marcus, wanted in. Fearing ulterior motives, Numerian initially denied Gnaeus that affiliation. An outraged Gnaeus began a rumor that Numerian was in a conspiracy with Rome. It was never proven, but it is suspected that Gnaeus thus engineered the assassination of Numerian. People say that move against Numerian was to show the Senators of Rome just how powerful Gnaeus was. That not even the Emperor of Rome was safe from his reach.

"With Numerian out of the picture, Gnaeus campaigned again for membership in Legacy. Though, the Senators held steadfast to the words of their slaughtered Emperor. So Gnaeus bought his way in--and where Rome had begun with one sect, there now were two.

"Gnaeus formed what was originally known as Inferna Discipulis, or "Hell's Disciples." He offered a lot of money to anyone who joined his ranks. His last will and testament stipulated that only a Crassus would, forever, control Inferna Discipulis. Suspecting he was going to the underworld anyway, the name was changed to Crassus. Gnaeus wanted the sect to be synonymous with hell."

Shields starts to tell me about his history with Lazarus. "After my final Proelium, Lazarus tried to kill me. I left the arena and was walking through the Sphere. I had defeated a Crassus fighter and retained my place as the champion of Legacy. Lazarus didn't accept the win. As he saw it, I was supposed to fall in battle. He came at me from behind and stabbed me, puncturing a lung and just missing my heart.

Guards saw the commotion and apprehended him before I could get a chance. He was never reprimanded for that act--he just made a large endowment to the Assembly, and all was forgiven. But I will wreak my vengeance before I meet my death."

His steely eyes lock on mine, and I feel their lucid energy sink deep into me. I've never seen this side of Shields before. I've only known him to be unwavering.

"Beware of him. You are a threat to him, young man. Now that he knows you are the Echo of Spartacus, it's not unlikely that he will try to have you killed. He is a snake in the grass. If he can't get to you, he will find a way to bring you to him."

Crassus doesn't know where I live, I thought, and they wouldn't be stupid enough to try anything at Aurelius. I was okay--McKenna was my only concern, but she was rarely out of my sight. I welcome Crassus' ambitions--and besides, Owen and I have unfinished business, and I am going to settle what he started.

CHAPTER 5: MCKENNA

I left Luke at the apartment that morning. Juliet and I wanted to have some girl time. She was the only real friend I'd made at school. I was enjoying myself, but between that and Luke I didn't have time to meet new people-- not that I really cared to. Luckily, Juliet was Luke's best friend's girlfriend. It made things so much easier having another couple to be friends with.

I drove over to Juliet's dorm room. We were going shopping, so I'd taken the car for the day.

When I got there, she was waiting outside for me. She hopped in, and I could tell from her smile she was excited to get out.

"Hey, how *are* you?" I asked.

"I'm *good*. Still a little on edge from last night. I

needed this time."

She had come to the Proelium with Bobby and me-- her first time going, even though this is Linc's second year fighting in Legacy. Juliet is a sweet girl. She isn't into all of this fighting stuff. She's so worried about Linc every time he fights. I'm an army brat, so I'm no stranger to combat; that's why I don't get nervous watching Luke. He's a great fighter, probably the best I've ever seen. He taught me how to protect myself. Even though we do everything together, he wanted to feel confident that, if for any reason he wasn't around, I could ward off an attacker.

"So, Jules, how are you and Linc?"

"We're good, couldn't be better. We're going up to Vermont for the weekend. We both love snow boarding, so we figured we might as well make the trip while we have the time. You and Luke should come with us!"

Winter sports weren't really big for Luke and me. We liked to watch the winter X-Games when they were on, but that's not something we would actually like to do. I know personally I would rather be hot than cold.

"That's so nice, but we wouldn't want to impose," I said. "Besides, Luke and I are more warm weather types."

"No worries--not too many people like the snow. . . This is a really nice car, by the way."

"Thanks. Luke loves it, probably almost as much as me!" I joked.

"Do you think he'd mind if I drove it?"

I didn't have a problem with that, and I knew Luke wouldn't mind either. "Sure," I said, and pulled over to the curb. I wasn't expecting what happened next.

"Wow, this car is ridiculous!" she said. "A Challenger SRT8--392-inch engine displacement, 6.4 litter Hemi, pushing 470 horses, and 6-speed manual transmission. This car does 0 to 60 in 4.5 seconds."

I'd had no idea--been under the impression that she was just a nice sweet girl. "I didn't know you knew about cars," I said.

"Yeah. Linc doesn't even know. It's kind of a secret. My dad used to own a shop. Every day after school I'd go there and he'd teach me about cars. He would've killed for a car like this! We used to go to car shows together all the time. He always said one day he'd buy a junker '71 Dodge Challenger and rebuild it."

"That's so great! Has he found one yet?"

"No, he hasn't, and he won't be able to now. My father passed away two years ago."

"I'm so sorry. I had no idea."

"It's okay. My dad was sick. I was actually happy when he went, because he didn't have to suffer anymore."

"What, uh, what did he have, if you don't mind my asking."

"Huntington's chorea. A neurodegenerative genetic disorder. Incurable--it slowly kills by breaking down the brain until you cease to function. There's a 50/50 chance a child will develop it if a parent has. Luckily, I tested negative... I was heartbroken when he died. He was my best friend. I went to a dark place after, pretty much closed myself off from the world, from people. And then, a few months later, the guy of my dreams fell in love with me--and he reminds me a lot of my dad."

"That's why I get so nervous about watching him fight. I know Linc is a good fighter, he can handle his end, but I can't help it. I would go insane if he got hurt really badly or worse. I watched my dad die for ten years. I don't think I could deal with it a second time."

My heart had sunk when she told me about her father. How *do* you cope with losing a true love, the only part of you that makes you whole.

The dark mood had passed by the time we reached the mall. We found as close of a spot to the entrance as we could and went in. Neither one of us had anything in mind to buy. We liked simply walking around and talking.

"Hey," she said, "I have to go to the bathroom really quick."

Waiting for her, I couldn't stop thinking about our conversation in the car. I loved my family, but I couldn't fathom losing Luke. He is my *compagnion d'âme*, Tristan to my Isolde, my best friend. I was having fun with Jules, but I missed Luke. It's not the same hanging out with your girl friends when your lover is your best friend. I was looking forward to getting back to him and sent him a text: *What are you doing? I love you.*

While waiting for him to text back, I couldn't help but notice a glimmer in the store window I was leaning against. I peered in to get a better look. It was an engagement ring with a round central cluster of diamonds.

I had never asked the question, but I could definitely see myself marrying Luke. There was no doubt that we belonged together--we'd been attached at the hip for so long by then. I guess I was nervous bringing it up because I didn't know how Luke would react. What if he didn't want to. . . ? I'd feel like a fool. I would marry him tomorrow if he wanted.

"Okay, I'm back. You wouldn't *believe* the line in there. What you looking at?" Juliet asked.

"This little engagement ring. Just a thought."

"Mrs. Luke Hart? Mrs. McKenna Hart? Sounds fantastic to *me*. You guys were *made* for each other. I just know I better be the maid of honor when it happens!"

But I knew I'd never have an answer if I didn't bring

up the subject with Luke. I promised myself I'd talk to him soon.

We left the mall and headed home. We got hungry, so we stopped at a great burger joint she knew not far from campus. We thought the boys might be hungry, so we ordered them a couple of burgers too, all to go. We'd already left the place when Juliet sighed, "Damn it! I think I left my phone inside. Wait one second while I go and find it?"

"Yeah, no problem." While I waited, I checked my own phone to see if Luke had texted back. There was one new message: *I love you, too. The meeting was interesting. Tell you about it when you get home.*

I wondered what was so interesting and had opened my purse to put my phone away when I was approached by four guys, two of whom stopped right in front of me.

"Excuse me?" I said.

"Hey, hottie--nice car. Why don't you let me drive you around, huh? I can give you a great ride."

"Back off," I said. "I'm warning you."

"*Warning* me? You're not going to do anything. I

was trying to be nice, but I don't have to be. You should be begging to come with me."

The guy grabbed my forearm. I snatched it away, wishing Luke was there. The guy continued to come at me.

"So what's it going to be? You gonna beg like a good little girl, or am I just going to have to take what I want from you?"

Out of nowhere, I heard a voice say, "She isn't going to be begging for anything." It was Owen, the guy Luke was going to fight in Haze. What was he doing there? And why was he helping me?

"This is no business of yours," the guy said.

"I'm making it my business. Four of you against her. . . doesn't seem fair to me. Why don't we even the odds a bit? How about you four versus me?" Owen offered

The guy harassing me hesitated. He wanted to take the chance but backed down. His friends seemed to share his feelings, because they started backing away as well.

Owen watched them until they turned the

corner. "You okay?" he asked me.

"I'm fine. Thanks for helping me."

He raised a finger. ". . .I know you. You were at Haze a while back. You're Luke's girl."

"Yes, I am. He'd be grateful to you, too."

"Save it. I didn't do it for him. Luke and I still have unfinished business. This was a separate matter. You're his girl, and your loyalty should lie with him. I won't stand by and watch some thugs threaten a defenseless woman."

"I'm not defenseless. I can take care of myself, and I don't recall having asked for help!"

"Please. Even if you did ward one off, maybe even two, there's no way you could've handled four of them. Whether you asked for it or not, you needed my help, and I saved your ass. So say thank you."

"I'm not saying thank you." I said.

"McKenna, what's going on?" Juliet asked. She'd finally found her phone.

"Nothing, he was just leaving."

Owen turned away. What was his issue? If he had a problem with me because of Luke, why help me? I was perfectly capable of handling myself.

"Really?" she said. "When I found my phone, I looked out the window and saw Owen standing next you. What'd he want?"

"Nothing. These jerks were harassing me, and he made them leave."

"Owen is not a good person. That night in Haze, he only came in to start a fight. He and his friends had no right being there."

". . .What do you know about him?"

"All I know is what Linc's told me and what one of my friends said. After the party Linc was going on about how Nikko should've fought Owen then and there. Apparently, Nikko and Owen have known each other for a long time and got into an altercation outside the arena. Linc said that Owen's killed more people in Legacy than anyone else."

"What about your friend? What did he say?"

"She," Juliet pointed out. She used to date him not too long ago. She said that he was arrogant, neglecting, and abusive. He would verbally rip into her, and one night she showed up at my door distraught. They'd gotten into an argument, and Owen had hit her. She tried to press charges, but the cops wouldn't pursue it. She left school a week after it happened."

Then why would he help me? It wasn't that big a deal, but I listened to what Juliet had to say. Hopefully I wouldn't run into him by myself again.

We got into the car. I dropped her off at her dorm and then went home.

Luke had already gotten back. When I came in, he had music blasting and was working out in the living room. I said, "Hey," as I walked in.

He stopped what he was doing and rose to greet me. He was wearing shorts, and sweat was dripping down his chest. I have to admit I still get excited when I see him looking so powerful --the veins in his biceps popping out, his pronounced pects and tight six-pack, unshaven beard, tattoos--I love all of him.

I know it might seem strange, but the few hours I had been away from him were too long. I hurried over to him and fell into his arms. It's not the same going places without him. He makes me feel safe, understands me, and doesn't judge.

"How's Jules?" he asked.

"She's good. We had a nice time today. We really connected, and we've become closer. Juliet invited us to Vermont this weekend. She and Linc are going snowboarding while they have time."

"That was nice of her," he said, "but I'm not a big fan of the cold."

I smiled.

I started to tell him about what had happened earlier with Owen. Before I could get it out, though, he started talking about his meeting at Aurelius.

"I met Bobby's father, Thomas Goodwin. He and Professor Shields have been friends for ages. Shields wanted me to meet him. Mr. Goodwin is a big part of Aurelius. While we were talking, the head of Crassus barged into Shields' office unannounced. His name is Lazarus Caius Crassus. Goodwin and Shields warned me that Lazarus most likely wants to see me dead because of my blood history. They said that, long ago, his ancestor was given the task of killing Spartacus and failed. Now that he knows I'm the Echo, Lazarus thinks he can redeem his ancestor's honor. I don't want you to worry, but it would be wrong for me to keep this from you. Lazarus Crassus is a callous individual, and it's possible he may go as far as to try and get to me by coming after you. I've never lied to you, and I'm not going to start now. You deserved to know, but I promise I will lay down my life making sure no harm ever comes your way."

The assurance and softness in his voice were genuine. I know it probably hadn't been easy to tell me that, but Luke was right--he didn't lie to me, and, after my encounter with Owen, I wasn't looking forward to going anywhere without Luke.

"I know," I said.

CHAPTER 6: THE CHAMPION OF LEGACY

The second Proelium is rapidly approaching. This time I've drawn the main event--my performance in the first Proelium was enough to confirm that I was indeed who they thought I was. I had fought like the true Echo of Spartacus. This time Shields takes it upon himself to prep me for the next fight. Since I began at Aurelius, he has become a mentor to me. There is no better person for the role than him. For the first Proelium, he left Bobby in charge of prepping me. This time he wants to do it himself.

"How do you feel about vampires?" Shields asks me.

"I. . .I've never really thought much about them. I guess I'd have to say I'm team Edward all the way."

"Bloody hell, no. What do you know about Dracula?"

"The usual. A fictional character created by Bram Stroker in 1897. The book became a cult classic and created an entire vampire-fan nation. He based the character on a real person named Vlad the Impaler."

Why is he asking me about this, though? Am I missing something? He didn't seem the bloodsucker type. Then it hit me.

"Don't tell me that's who I'm fighting."

"Good guess." He tosses me an old leather-bound book. "You will be facing Erno, the Bloodborn of Vladimir Tepes the Impaler."

"I'm fighting the Bloodborn of Dracula?"

"Vladimir Tepes III was a prince of Walachia in the 1500s. Many know him as Dracula. He received that name from his father, who served in the Order of the Dragon. Dragon in Romanian is Dracul. Thus Dracula--the son of the dragon. The Order was founded at the time of the Crusades. They vowed to defend Christianity and the symbol of the cross from the Ottomans. It was a monarchic order of chivalry, a fellowship of knights."

Shields sat me down across from him and explains, "Vladimir's infamous reputation rests on the sadistic behavior he exhibited. Battling the Ottomans mainly, he used impalement as a form of torture. Some say Vlad drank the blood of his victims. His cruelty had no bounds, and, if the reports are to be believed, he claimed upwards of eighty to a hundred thousand victims. Someone eventually assassinated him, ironically by a stake through the heart.

"You'd think, with the blood lust Erno has, he'd be an Echo. He's very skilled with a weapon and very eccentric. Erno tries to impale his opponents during a fight and cleans his blade by liking off the blood. He fights with the sword of Vladimir Tepes. That weapon, the kilij, is a single-edged sword, and it will give you a bad time if he manages to strike you cleanly with it. We need to continue to improve your sword skill. Erno will be gunning for a chance to taste your blood. He's one of Ares's Worshipers. They pray to the Greek god of war, Ares, the son of Zeus and Hera. Members of that house are usually very violent. Mars was the Roman equivalent of the Greek god, but, unlike Ares, he created the Roman people."

Shields and I head to the training room. We are in there working for hours. I had been able to get past Baldr in the first Proelium with my rudimentary sword abilities, but I wouldn't be able to pull off the same trick twice. I had to unlock more of my connection with Spartacus. The memories came randomly and never often enough. I had become a better fighter after I trained on his memories in the Arsenal. Maybe, I told myself, that's the key I'm missing.

So, I need to train in the Arsenal, perhaps because I am surrounded by so much history and residual energy tied to the weapons it makes it easier for Spartacus to come through. Whatever the reason, I know I have to get back there.

I tell Shields my plan of training in the Arsenal. I wanted to run the idea past him since there are so many valuable items inside.

Shields agrees to let me use the room, "Just don't break anything--the items in that room are worth more than you."

He shows me back down the corridor. The fire of Aurelius is still burning as high and bright as it had been the first time I visited the room. Once we enter, he pauses before the mark to pay his respects to the man the sect is named after.

"Doors open or closed?" he asks over his shoulder as he leaves me in peace.

"Open."

"I'll let you get to it, then. Lock up on your way out."

When he is gone, I take up a position in the middle of the room with my eyes closed, envisioning Spartacus. I try to put myself back in the same time as when I first experienced him. To my surprise, the memories started again, just as I hoped they would. Once I am Spartacus, I am ready to begin. This time he is fighting two people in the arena. I embrace the memory and allow myself to be totally taken over in an otherworldly possession. Totally under the control of the memory. My body is moving voluntarily to the sight of the past. Though there is no one else in the room, just me being influenced by my Origin. I did this as a way to activate my muscle memory. So I would feel the movements and apply them in my training-- and in battle.

The memory lasts until Spartacus wins the fight. When I came out of the trance, I had another new scar, this time across my forearm. McKenna won't be happy with this. It is still crazy to think that I am so connected to Spartacus that I can physically manifest through genetic memories.

Two hours have passed since I've begun connecting to Spartacus. I am tremendously fatigued and eager to lie down. I drive back to the apartment, where I find McKenna asleep on the couch. The TV is on, and her hands still in a typing position on her laptop. I move the computer out of the way, scoop her into my arms, and carry her to bed. She must have had a long day because she doesn't even notice me moving her.

I pull the covers over her, tuck her in, and go back out to the living room to turn everything off before I go to bed myself. Since the TV is still on, I start to watch it for a few minutes. I like the show that is on. McKenna's laptop is still open, and the screen has woken up since I moved it. The brightness is blinding; as I reach to turn it off, I notice something interesting-a jewelry website open to an engagement ring. I don't know what to think at first. Does she want to get married? My heart starts to race, and an overwhelming feeling of happiness comes over me. From the first moment I saw her, it's always been my intention to marry McKenna. I guess I'd gotten so caught up in how perfect we already were together that the thought had slipped my mind. In my eyes, we are already married. It's the first time, at least that I am aware of, McKenna has ever considered the subject.

I know what I am going to do.

I shut the laptop, turn off the TV, and go to bed. As exhausted as I am since the training session ended, a goodnight's sleep is just what I need.

When I get to Shields' class the following day, Bobby is sitting outside waiting for me. Unfortunately, I am a bit late, which is why I find it strange; Bobby is not inside?

"He canceled today," Bobby says. "I wonder what's going on."

I have no idea. The man is never late or misses anything, but class is canceled. That means I don't have to sit through another one of his lectures that day. They are often longer than I can bear staying awake for.

"I don't know," I reply. "Let's get out of here. We'll figure it out later." Bobby and I decided to head back through campus.

"I met your dad the other day, by the way--really great guy," I say.

"Thanks. My dad is pretty cool, isn't he? He's great to hang out with, and he's doing a good job getting me ready to join him as co-historian. He says Aurelius would be even better if we worked together."

"That's great, bro--I'm happy for you. I almost forgot! How did things end up going with Kanae?"

"She hasn't been in class the last couple of days. I haven't seen her--"

Bobby suddenly stops in his tracks. "Right there!"

He shouts.

"Right where? What am I supposed to be looking at?"

"Right there, man! There she is. I'm going. Hold my stuff real quick, just one second. Hold my stuff." Bobby hands me his bag and goes after her, determined to have a conversation with her, but I can tell he is still nervous. He runs a hand through his hair and tucks his shirt in all the way before he reaches her. Bobby taps Kanae on her shoulder, and she turns around.

"Hey, umm, hi--excuse me," he says awkwardly.

"Hey, Bobby, how are you?"

"I'm good, you know, just working hard and other stuff--you know how it is."

Kanae laughs at his anxious banter. "That's good."

"I haven't seen you in class lately. I miss seeing you for an hour and a half every Monday, Wednesday, and Thursday at 9:30 am."

"Yeah, I know. I was away. Family issues."

He isn't as awkward as I expected him to be. He's keeping eye contact, isn't stuttering much, and has kept her engaged in the conversation.

"So, what kind of stuff do you do?" Kanae asks.

"Uh, well, you know, I work, hang out with my friends, and go to parties. Just try to keep busy. I don't have anyone, well, like a significant other, a girlfriend. I'm single, is what I'm trying to say. It gets lonely sometimes, but I'm waiting for the right one. I don't want to tie myself down until I find her."

"I know what you mean. I don't have anyone either. Where do you party? I like to go out, but there's nobody for me to go out with."

"You don't say. What--uh, what are your plans for tonight? Are you busy?"

"No, I'm free."

"Would you like to go out with me? My friend over there, his girlfriend, and another couple of friends of ours, we're all going to Haze. A mutual friend is hosting a party--do you know Nikko?"

"Not personally, but I know who he is."

"Good, well, it's his party, and I would love it if you would join me."

"Yes. I'd love to go out with you!" She pulled out a sheet from a notepad and a pen from the tote bag she's carrying, writes her number down, and tells Bobby to call her later with the details.

"Tote bag? You must have a lot of things in there." Bobby jokes.

"Yeah, I have a few personal things... See you tonight, Bobby."

He was right--she is classically beautiful. I'm not sure if he told me, but she looks like she is of Asian descent, maybe Japanese? She has long highlighted brown hair, perfect skin, and her eyes are captivating.

"Did you see that?" he asks, proud of himself for being brave enough to talk to her. "Tell me you saw that! What did I tell you, huh? She is a goddess!"

"Yeah, man. So you told Kanae we're all going to Haze tonight? What happened to discretion? That is an Aurelius club. How do you explain that?"

"No worries--I'll just tell her it's a frat. But, did you see her? Screw Legacy! It will be great."

Later that night, we are all sitting in VIP, waiting for Bobby and Kanae. McKenna and Juliet don't want to dance until they meet Kanae. They couldn't believe it when I told them about her. They might be more excited for Bobby than he is for himself.

"Where are they?" Juliet demands.

"She probably stood him up. I know I would if I was her," Linc jokes, refusing to believe Bobby could have landed a date with a hot girl.

"That's mean," McKenna says, defending our late friend. "Bobby isn't a bad-looking guy at all, and he's nice. He deserves a great girl."

Just then, I spot the two walking hand in hand through the crowd. Bobby is leading her over. He looks happy; I had never seen that expression on his face, so proud to have Kanae on his arm.

Finally, in our section, Bobby makes the introductions.

"Hi, everyone," Kanae says. "Bobby's told me so much about you."

We saved them room to sit down. The two join our little party, and we begin to get to know the new addition to our group.

Kanae seems to fit right in; McKenna and Juliet quickly take a liking to her.

Nikko takes the microphone and asks the room for quiet. The music stops, and silence falls over the crowd. We all look to Nikko to see what he is going to say.

"Good evening, and welcome to Haze. Before we really start partying the night away, I'd like to take the time to acknowledge a few people in the club tonight. To my brothers in arms, may we continue to find glory and honor. We pray to the gods for another victory in the second Proelium. So raise your glasses and drink for the moment--and if you don't have a glass, have one on me. For the brotherhood!"

"For Aurelius!" The room responds.

The music comes back on, and the party starts again. People are soon dancing and having a good time. McKenna and I dance for a while, and when we begin to get tired, return to the VIP section to sit down.

"Look at Bobby and Kanae--he looks so happy," she says to me. "What do you think about her?"

"I think she's great. She's so nice and funny. Perfect for Bobby. I'm happy for him. She's going to fit in perfectly."

McKenna and I leave early--I need to get some rest. The Proelium is just two days away, and I can't spend my energy before the main event.

The days fly by fast, almost as if I had fallen asleep and woken up in the Sphere. The arena is packed; there's not an empty seat in the house. The cheering is so loud that the sound resonates through our barracks.

Bobby's father comes to speak to me before we leave the dressing area. He has a strange look on his face.

"You ready for this fight?" Goodwin asks.

"Of course. Erno stands no chance."

"Good. Stay on your toes. I've been--well, there's no easy way to put this, son. I've heard rumors that Crassus has offered a large bounty for your death. Over the years, Ares Worshipers have often formed alliances with Crassus. So Erno will be gunning for you. He's already a blood-crazed maniac like his Origin, but now he has orders for your life."

Goodwin looks hard at me.

"What I'm saying is--fight to win, but don't hesitate to take his life if you have to."

So Crassus wants me dead already. That's fine--he is going to have to do better than sending Dracula's Bloodborn after me. I don't show it, but I am livid. My body grows restless as I wait to enter. If Crassus really wants me gone, I will have to show him just how tough it will be to make that happen.

Linc goes first, battling the Bloodborn of Spiculus. The gladiator who once gained the admiration of the infamous Emperor Nero. The fight lasts a while. The guy isn't bad, but Linc has improved immensely and is determined to win; his opponent could only hold him off for so long.

Nikko fights second for Aurelius, and, as expected, he wins his match. He doesn't have flair, but he doesn't make mistakes either, and he's strong as an ox and quick on his feet. He's not in it for the praise of the crowd, though they certainly give it when he wins.

They have set a good tempo for me. My gear is on, the red strip of McKenna's dress again tied to my hand.

The third match has ended, and I am now waiting in the darkness of the entry ramp.

The Master of Ceremonies quiets the crowd. "The Ares Worshipers deliver a gift in the form of a true warrior. Tonight, we are in the presence of legend and myth. I give to you Erno, the Bloodborn of Vladimir Tepes the Impaler, Dracula."

A low whisper runs through the crowd: They see him as the Bloodborn of Dracula, not of the torturer of many thousands. But, the fans believe what they are being sold. So, now it's my turn to go out and drive my steel through his heart.

When the Master of Ceremonies begins to speak again, the crowd erupts in excitement, knowing I will appear from the darkness behind the gate. Finally, they compose themselves long enough for the Master of Ceremonies to announce me. "Ladies and gentlemen, witness a gladiator who needs no introduction. The Echo of Spartacus, Luke, the Decimator of Baldr."

I am all business, marching with my double blades at my side to the center of the arena. I bow my head and raise my sword to acknowledge the crowd. When I peer up, I notice that everyone in the stands has a red ribbon tied around their hands just as I do. They raise those red fists with me as a sign of respect.

Erno slightly resembles the depictions of Vlad III. Black hair, a long nose, and dark eyebrows. He has the kilij in his left hand and a halberd in the right. I know he will use that long ax to try to drive it through me if he gets the opportunity.

There is no talk. We just begin fighting. Erno doesn't attack much with kilij; he is using it more to deflect my advances. The halberd is his primary weapon; the ax gives him the chance to strike a blow from a greater distance. I recognize he doesn't want to get too close to me. Every thrust of the halberd is aimed at my head, or he uses the tip to try and impale me. I'm going to have to try to get it out of his hand. My swords serve for close combat, and I am at a disadvantage as long as he holds onto both weapons.

Erno lands an unexpected blow to my quad that sent me momentarily to one knee. The pain is searing--it is the first time I have ever taken a strike like that.

Erno retreats while I am still down, enjoying watching me suffer. It's like he's getting off on it. He stares at the blood dripping from the edge of the halberd. His hand is covered in it.

"The blood of the Echo," he murmurs raising the bloody hand to his face to examine it more closely. He takes in the scent and then licks it off.

"The taste is tremendous!" he barks in a hoarse voice. "I enjoy drinking it. Give me more!"

Erno begins to advance on me. I block the thrust of the halberd this time, sliding backward and sidestepping the return sweep. He moves instinctively with me; I raise the short sword in my left from that near-impossible stance with my weight on my right leg and successfully slice his left bicep nearly in half. His arm falls, immobile. Erno swings the halberd twice more, not blindly but overcome by pain; there is no technique in his attempts. I avoid each attack and become furious that he had landed the blow to my leg. The pain is hindering my movement.

He swings the halberd at my head once more; I

deflect the blow, shift quickly, and with lightning speed raise my sword above my shoulder, and bring it down with all the weight of my shoulder and leg behind it, severing his hand. Erno shrieks, and the halberd clatters to the sand in an abstract spray of blood.

Erno hesitates as he realizes he only has one hand left. I swing my blade at him again and relieve him of the other. Blood pours like water from a faucet as he falls to his knees and begins to pass out. I decide to spare his life, not because I am merciful, but because he is to be a sufferer in my cause--and Lazarus can now see that perhaps his course of action just might unleash an absolute monster.

I salute the crowd again by raising my fist. My business is done in the arena tonight. It's time to return to the darkness.

CHAPTER 7: A LITTLE TIME OFF

The year is going by fast. It's been several weeks since my fight against Erno. I have continued my training, but winter break has arrived; it's time for McKenna and me to take some much-needed time away from Legacy.

We haven't decided what we want to do--go home and see our families or spend the time cuddled up in the apartment watching Christmas movies.

Time off is, in any case, literally what the doctor has ordered. After the halberd blow, I needed 120 stitches to my wounded leg--three layers of twenty-five each to repair the muscle and another forty-five to close the skin. I had healed, but the wound had left a sickening scar.

The fighting is starting to take a toll on McKenna, too. She is into the competition, but seeing me risk life and limb is sometimes too much for her to handle.

Since the next Proelium isn't scheduled to occur until after New Year's, I will focus all my energy on her. Christmas is her favorite holiday--the gift-giving, and the general brightness of the joy around, captivate McKenna's spirit.

I haven't heard any rumors of Crassus plotting against me since Goodwin warned me about Erno. I suspect the allied force of the House of Crassus and Ares Worshipers have received my rebuttal message to their plot. I don't know how long until they will back down, if at all, but for now, at least death is taking a holiday.

"So, stud, what's the plan for Christmas?" McKenna asks.

"It's not that big of a deal for me. What would you like to do?"

"My mom tells me they're going away for the holidays, and so are your parents. So, I think we should stay here and celebrate together, just the two of us."

"You got it!" McKenna has already started decorating the apartment. I've just been sitting around, watching her in the swing of things. It's been snowing outside for hours, so there's not much else to do.

"Something is missing." She says, standing in the entryway to the living room. Pondering over the decor.

"We need a tree! A tree," McKenna insists.

So, we venture out into the snow to find one. McKenna is enjoying herself drinking hot cocoa and singing along to the Christmas songs on the radio. Winter storms like this are the one time I regret not having a truck. I can barely see, and I am blasting the windshield with the defroster to try and clear up the fog covering the window. I love to drive, but this is insane. There are no shops open. Every place we pass has a sign that says, we're closed.

After driving around for an hour, we finally find a parking lot where Christmas trees are on sale. This place has hundreds of trees ready for picking. We rummage around for a while because McKenna can't decide which she wanted.

"What do you think--the seven-foot or the eight?" she asks.

"What about this one right here? It has character." I point to a tiny Charlie Brown tree lying on the ground.

"You're a comedian now? A hilarious multi-talented fighter! Bravo. . . I'm serious, Luke. Which one?"

The eight is too tall for the apartment, and we would have had to move things around to boot because it is so full. "I like the seven-foot."

She doesn't take my advice. We pay for the eight-footer and strap it to the roof of the car.

It is quite the task of getting the thing up the stairs, but I manage. I hate to admit this, but Mckenna was right--the tree looks great. I start to get in the spirit of things when I see it standing in place. We decorate it together and then as plannned cuddle up on the couch watching Christmas movies until we fall asleep.

We spend the next few days getting our gifts together for each other. I have big presents for

McKenna, and I hope she likes them. We decide not to open anything until Christmas morning. It is hard hiding my gifts from her. She is like a kid snooping around, trying to sneak a peek.

We spend Christmas Eve with Juliet, Linc, Bobby, and Kanae -- we have them over for dinner and hang out a while before they all head back to their homes to bring in the day. The night was fun. We played cliché games and told relationship stories until we were all ready to hit the sack.

Bobby and Kanae had become official shortly after their first date, and he couldn't be happier. His father likes her, too. Bobby had felt he was incapable of finding love, but love isn't about how you seem to yourself, but about how another person sees who you really are. They look at you and don't register flaws or imperfections. They see perfection in the beauty that is you and love the happiness you give them.

When Christmas morning comes, it is exciting to see all the presents under the tree. McKenna's gifts are great--she has bought me nice clothes, a new computer, and headphones. I love the gifts. She always took the time to buy me things that she knew I would enjoy.

I ask McKenna to sit down on the couch.

"Well, where's it at?" She asks.

"Close your eyes first."

I had hidden her gift in the kitchen earlier this morning. While her eyes are closed, I run to the kitchen to grab her present. I gently place the gift in her arms. "Okay, you can open them now."

McKenna opens her eyes to find a large red box with a white bow. The lid had holes in it and starts shaking as she picks it up.

"What is it?" McKenna wonders.

"Open it and find out."

She lifts the top off the box, and a smile shot across her face. "No way! When did you...?"

An all-white German shepherd puppy pops out of the box and kisses her on the nose. The handsome little dog's ears are standing straight up, and he has ghostly blue eyes. Growing up, McKenna had always wanted a dog but had never been allowed to have one. I've wanted a puppy of my own, too.

"Oh my god, he is too cute! What are we going to name him?" she asks.

"I don't know--he's your Christmas gift. What do you think?"

"How about we call you Luka? Luka shall be your name."

I loved it--an epic name. Before she got too preoccupied with the puppy, I had to turn her attention to my two other presents. "Ready for your next gift?"

"There's more?"

I reach into my back pocket, pull out her second gift, and set it down on the table in front of her. She puts the puppy down long enough for me to get out what I have to say.

"Hugh Walpole once wrote, *'The most wonderful of all things in life, I believe, is the discovery of another human being with whom one's relationship has a glowing depth, beauty, and joy as the year's increase. This inner progressiveness of love between two human beings is a most marvelous thing, it cannot be found by looking for it or by passionately wishing for it. It is a sort of Divine accident.*' Three years ago, fate brought us to the same place and time. So that we could be together. I'm happy with you being my girlfriend...but I would be honored if you would be my wife."

I present McKenna with a small black box. She grabs

it from me and opens it to find the 18-carat white gold vintage engagement ring. The ring I thought suited her the best, with a center stone a little over a carat, accented by six round sapphires and framed by forty-eight pavé-set round diamonds with filigree detailing.

The gesture takes her breath away. Tears run down her face, and she covers her mouth, trying to find the words to express what she was feeling. I take her hand and study her bare finger for the last time. I remove the ring from the box and slide it onto her left ring finger. The color of the metal flatters her skin tone. She stretches out her hand and admires the ring, her breaths slow, almost as if she is trying to comprehend the reality of the situation.

"Yes, of course, I will--but how did you know?" She

finally asks.

"It doesn't matter how I knew. All that matters is that I can't go on without calling you, my wife."

"This is the best Christmas ever."

"Well, it's not over yet."

"What do you mean? There can't possibly be more." I hand her an envelope--my most spontaneous gift.

"What is this?" McKenna asks.

"Christmas together is perfect, but how do you feel about bringing in the New Year in Las Vegas?"

"Vegas?" McKenna is elated to find two round-trip tickets, and she can't decide which gift she is more excited about.

"Look, Luka, Mommy, and Daddy are going to Las Vegas! Wait --who's going to look after Luka while we're gone?"

"Don't worry about that. Bobby said he'd come over and watch Luka. Three days in Vegas--what could be better?"

"This is really too much, Luke. I would've been happy with just the puppy. This Christmas is definitely a dream come true. Thank you!"

It's hard to express my feelings from seeing her as my fiancée and not my girlfriend. I feel proud, blissful. She has honored me with that one word more than the applause of any crowd.

We spend the next couple of days packing for the trip. Soon, it is time to head to the airport. I have another surprise awaiting McKenna on our arrival.

"Come on, Luke, we have to hurry up and get the gate."

"There's no rush--we're already through the security check, and our flight doesn't leave for another hour and a half." In her excitement, she has neglected to actually check our flight time.

At the gate, McKenna sees her surprise. "No way!" she cries as she runs ahead of me. Standing at our gate, holding a big sign that read Vegas, are Juliet and Linc. I told them I wanted to take McKenna away for the New Year, and they said they would come.

"What are you guys doing here?" she exclaims.

"We're going to Vegas!" Juliet says. "There's no way we were going to let you go without us."

Linc adds, "Luke told us that he planned something special for you and invited us to tag along."

McKenna turns to me and throws her arms around my neck. She stares into my eyes and kisses me.

"You did this all for me?" she asks.

"I'd do anything for you."

"This is going to be the best trip ever!" McKenna declares.

We board an hour later, with Linc and Juliet sitting right behind us. I look out the window at all the snow as the plane makes its way to the runway.

The flight to Las Vegas from New York is about six hours. After sitting on the tarmac, the pilot is finally cleared for takeoff. Shortly after we are in the air, I fall asleep for the entire flight. McKenna wakes me up as we began our descent into Vegas, Nevada. I open my eyes to the lights of the Vegas Strip illuminating the night sky. The pilot announces that the temperature on the ground is in the upper 80s at 8 o'clock at night.

Since we are only staying three days and two nights, we have only brought carry-on bags. We all pile into a shuttle and head for the Palms Casino and Resort when we got off the plane. Since it's New Year's in Vegas, the hotel only had suites left, so I had reserved the G-Suite for us all to stay in.

The heat is barely bearable even at night. But seeing all the attractions and lights as we drove up the boulevard kept me distracted from the uncomfortable warmth.

The lights, and energy of the hotel, are brilliant. We are going to have a great time. After check-in, we take the elevator up to our room.

"Whoa, this place is ridiculous!" Linc exclaims.

"It's gorgeous--but can you afford it?" McKenna asks.

"No sweat," I assure her. "Let me deal with that. We have three days! What are we going to do first?"

The Christmas gifts and the trip had been expensive, but I had a lot of money stashed away. I had taken a lot of fights before I moved back to the U.S. I knew no one could defeat me, so I'd bet on myself each time. Since I was only seventeen and a foreigner, I'd usually fought as the underdog against one-sided bets, so I very quickly made more money than I knew what to do with.

My efforts have succeeded, and McKenna soon goes back to enjoying herself. We clean up and head out for the night. Nothing could've made this night any better--good friends and my fiancée by my side.

The following day, Linc and I wake up early to run a few errands. I have arranged for McKenna and Juliet to have a day of pampering. Before I left this morning, I place a note on the pillow next to where McKenna is sleeping:

Good morning, my gorgeous fiancée. Hope you slept well. Linc and I ran out to pick up a few things, but have no fear--you won't suffer from boredom. We arranged for you and Jules to get the queen's treatment. Room service and the spa package will be there at 9:30. Be back soon.

I Love you.

I want New Year's Eve to be especially memorable. So, Linc helps me put together something huge I have planned. When we get back to the suite, the girls look refreshed and ready for the day.

"That was phenomenal!" McKenna says.

"Definitely," Juliet adds. "You two are working to get some tonight, aren't you?" Juliet jokes.

We get dressed and head out. It's only right that we see a show in Las Vegas, and Cirque Du Soleil is the one for us. The acrobatics, costumes, artistry, and creativity to produce a performance like that staggers the imagination.

Afterward, we stop back at the hotel to get ready for dinner. Linc and Juliet went to their room, and McKenna and I to ours.

"What is all this?" McKenna asks, stunned to see what is sitting on the bed--a pair of pear-shaped sapphire-and-diamond earrings in white gold, their vintage look the perfect complement to her engagement ring, and cobalt-blue satin stilettos.

The most noticeable item is the wedding gown-- a strapless ivory Maggie Sottero number with a crystal sash nestled beautifully beneath the sweeping neckline. The back is scooped and corseted with silk ties. The bubble hem train really gives the dress a flair that I thought McKenna would love.

She examines every item on the bed until she gets to the dress calling out to her from the bedspread. She runs her fingers down the fabric.

"I forgot to mention my resolution," I say from behind her. "It is New Year's Eve, after all. I vow to forever and always call you my wife--if you would do me the honor of marrying me." I got down on one knee.

With no hesitation in her voice, she looks down at me and says, "Yes."

Juliet and Linc are outside our door, listening in. They come running in to congratulate us as soon as McKenna says, yes.

"I'm so happy for you!" Juliet says. "There is no way I would miss out on being your maid of honor."

"Yeah, congratulations, guys," said Linc. "There isn't a better couple. Well, except us, of course."

This has been my plan all along. Starting the night, I saw the computer screen with the engagement ring.

Juliet helps McKenna get ready. Linc and I are out in the living room, getting dressed in classic black tuxedos, the only thing I would get married in.

Juliet comes out first to present McKenna. Juliet is wearing a stunning champagne one-sleeve dress Linc had bought her. "Presenting Mrs. McKenna Hart!" She says.

McKenna comes gliding through the bedroom door as if she had floated down from heaven. The dress hugs her body, accentuating every curve. Her hair is beveled and full of life. The chandelier earrings sparkle like stars in the night.

We head down to the front entrance of the Palms, where I have a limo waiting. People stare and clap as we cross the casino floor and lobby. Our union is being celebrated by a mass of avid supporters. We pile into the limo and are taken to the Stratosphere. I have arranged for us to get married there.

At the top of the building, we stand looking out the windows at the magic of the Vegas lights. It feels like we are on top of the world.

The pastor enters the room where we are waiting. "Are we ready?" He asks.

"Yes," I say, "we are."

McKenna and I walk in first to see the elaborately decorated room. There are flowers and candles all around. White satin cloths draped from the ceiling and the lights of the city as our backdrop.

I can tell McKenna is happy, but she has a gloomy look in her eyes. "What's wrong?"

"This is all so out of this world, but I really wish my parents and family could have been here."

"Well, I called both our parents, and they couldn't make it on such short notice. Don't worry, though-- your mother can see you right now; they're watching over a livestream as we speak."

"You really are perfect," she sighs.

I guess that tugged on the right heartstrings. McKenna promptly recomposes herself and is eager to get underway.

"I believe the groom has written his own vows?" the pastor asks.

I take McKenna by the hands and begin to recite what I have written:

"Save this night in memory. Look out into the night sky and see that the stars have aligned. Remember always a promise. Life was meaningless until I was blessed with the knowledge of your existence. Remember always a love living out the sands of time forever in your arms, transcending a time when our souls were but two halves of a whole searching for entirety. For tonight do we cement and honor a union long-established by our souls by joining everlastingly into holy matrimony."

McKenna can't hold back the tears. It is the first time she has ever really been at a loss for words.

The pastor proceeds, "Repeat after me. I, Luke, take you, McKenna, to be my wife, my life partner, and my one true love. I will cherish our friendship and love you today, tomorrow, and forever. I will love you faithfully through the best and the worst, through the difficult and the easy. As long as I am with you, harm shall never come your way. As I have given you my heart, so I give you my life to keep."

I repeat the words, and so does McKenna.

"By the power vested in me by the sovereign State of Nevada," said the pastor, "I now pronounce you husband and wife. You may kiss your bride!"

We kiss with a passion that burns hotter than twelve suns. I whisper, "Happy New Year!"

The clock strikes midnight, and the ball drops as we kiss. We are starting the New Year as husband and wife.

Juliet and Linc congratulate us and embrace us. We all leave the Stratosphere and go back to the hotel. The city streets are filled with excitement as everyone on the strip celebrates the new year. The Palms is one big party. We go back to the suite, Linc and Juliet depart to their room and McKenna and I to ours. I carry her across the threshold and lay her on the bed.

She wastes no time consummating the marriage.

CHAPTER 8: NEW REVELATIONS

A new year and I'm married, I thought. The trip had been phenomenal, but now we were back in the real world. The snow in Connecticut has melted from the streets, leaving only the chill and a white, dusty residue from the salted roads. Luka is excited to see us. Bobby has left a note listing what he'd done while we were gone:

Hey guys, congratulations on your marriage. Kanae and I watched the webcast. McKenna, you were stunning. I fed Luka earlier today. If you're reading this letter now, it means you're just getting home, so it's about time to feed him again. I'll see you guys later!

P.S. Luke, my dad, said he needs to talk to you. I don't know about what, but you might want to stop by and see what he wants.

I know Goodwin will be at Aurelius tomorrow, so I'll probably see him there.

"Hey, Luke, want to come with me to take Luka for a walk?" McKenna asks.

"Yeah, I do." I grab my coat and join her. We aren't outside too long--it's so cold, and we are both tired. When we get back, we immediately go to sleep.

The next day I stop by Shields' office after I have finished training for the day. The door is closed, so I knock. There is no reply. I tried twisting the knob, but the door is locked. It seems Shields is missing in action again. Usually, I wouldn't be concerned, but he has been so uncommonly secretive.

Goodwin spots me and wastes no time speaking to me. "We need to talk," he says. "Follow me."

I follow Goodwin to a part of Aurelius I hadn't seen before--a large, old room, like a library, with shelves of books everywhere, maps, and artifacts. Is this his office?

"Where are we?" I ask.

"It's called the Study. It's where the historians work. Every sect has one. These books are the records, recording every fighter's legends and historical facts ever known to history. I use them to follow bloodlines and discover new Bloodborns."

There are collections from floor to ceiling, and some so antiquated they are encased in glass cases to protect them from atmospheric damage. Goodwin has not brought me here for the view, though.

"What's going on?" I ask.

"Quite a display you put up against Erno--cutting off both his hands and then walking out of the arena?"

"I wanted to send Crassus a message."

"Well, you did that. The head of Ares Worshiper was livid with Lazarus, blamed him for the whole thing, and told him they were henceforth his adversaries."

I am happy with that. If Lazarus wants me dead, he is going to have to try harder.

"For the third Proelium, you'll be up against Ken Musashi," Goodwin says.

"Is there a problem with that?"

"Ken, like you, is an Echo--his Origin the most recognized samurai warrior of them all, Miyamoto Musashi. As I'm sure you know, samurai were chivalrous and honorable as a way of life. But they were fierce fighters in battle, known for their impeccable swordsmanship. And there was no one greater than Musashi."

"Did Lazarus hire him as well?"

"No. Ken is from the sect, Khan. Like us, they do not affiliate themselves with Crassus."

I want to know more about this man. The samurai were no people to take with a grain of salt, and if he is an Echo as well, I'll need a strategy to beat him. Part of that will be learning as much as possible to adapt if the fight starts going south.

"Tell me about him."

"Ken has been fighting in Legacy for three years now and has never lost. He fights like a demon. He's been up against every top dog in Legacy but Owen, and he's won every time."

"Why not Owen?" Three years and he's never met him in the arena; it's my understanding that Owen is the guy to beat.

"Ken and Owen were drawn to face each other twice, but Owen was switched out at the last minute on both occasions. For whatever reason, the Assembly decided that they will not fight each other."

So, either someone is under the impression that Owen would win or are afraid of Ken defeating him. Whatever--I need to focus on my fight.

"Musashi founded an entire school of swordsmanship known as Niten-ryū. He literally wrote the book on tactics, strategy, and philosophy-- The Book of Five Rings is still in use today. Musashi is a Kensei, a Legend, more or less, in English."

"What weapons does he use?"

"Ken fights only with a katana, the single-edge samurai sword and the sharpest weapon known to Legacy. The edge rivals that of a scalpel. People describe the edge of the blade as a cool sensation when it cleanly opens their skin. They only feel a cold touch as the blade passes. No one even knows they've been cut until they see the blood.

"The katana was, of course, used by Miyamoto Musashi. As legend has it, the Oni--demons, trolls, ogres, in Japanese culture, cursed the sword. They are invincible by nature, just as the blade is. Overall, the sword is forty-four inches long, the blade twenty-nine--which means, if you're not careful, Ken can and will strike you from a distance. You most likely won't even notice it until you realize you no longer have use of your limb."

Goodwin shuffles some papers on his desk before looking at me again, his gaze transparent and open. "I trust you will prepare. Ken is undefeated, but he is not undefeatable. He has weaknesses that you can use to your advantage. One avenue I think you should explore is fighting him hand to hand. Since he has been in Legacy, he has never fought without his sword--not that he needed to. If you can get the sword out of his hands, you'll shift the odds in your favor."

That is good to know. My sword skills wouldn't be able, it sounded to me, to match Ken's. I might struggle if I have to fight with weapons the whole time. But how will I get him to drop his sword and fight me unarmed?

"Who do I speak to about making a sizable bet on the fight?" I ask.

"You don't want to get mixed up with the people taking bets in Legacy. They're worse than the Camorra but call themselves 'influential members of the community.' I know some people making exclusive high-account wagers, though, and who are reliable. If you want, I can place your bet with them. Lord knows you don't need to make any more enemies. I'll find out what the odds are and let you know."

"Thank you."

"Don't worry about it. I've kept an eye on you so long; I feel like you're my own kid. Oh--and while you're here, you should check out this book." He hands me a leather-bound antiquarian volume. "Read it. You'll find out everything you could ever want to know about Spartacus."

I don't trust people easily, but Goodwin is different-- another father figure to me. I love my father and mother, but it's tough being so far away from my parents. I'm glad to know that Goodwin is around.

Once I finish up with Goodwin, I leave Aurelius and go back home. When I walk in, I see McKenna has left a note that she's taken Luka for a walk. I'm glad to see she is enjoying the puppy. I bought him to keep her company and feel like she has someone when I'm not around.

While I have time to kill, I decide I'll sit at the table and open Goodwin's book. There is so much about Spartacus in it I didn't know. Taking in the information makes me curious about something else: I leave the text on the table, open the laptop, and Google doppelgangers, a term sometimes used alternatively with "Echoes."

All my searches come back with similar results. Doppelgangers in folklore are paranormal doubles of a person; usually involved with malevolent forces, they signal danger or, if seen by their original, death. I do not know what the connection is. I know I am not evil, so what did that say about me?

I keep searching different forms of the word until one link catches my eye. The heading is *The Human Double.* I click on the link and start to read the page. The article speaks of the doppelganger as a re-embodiment-- a deceased progenitor's current form, not evil but reincarnations. It is common for the doppelganger to share physical characteristics and personality traits, and, under certain circumstances that generate vivid memories, the doppelganger would be an identical reoccurrence.

I look to see if there is any information on how to enhance this connection but found none. All I know is that training in the Arsenal caused me to have the memories. If I had to be the reincarnation of anyone, though, I am glad it's Spartacus.

McKenna comes through the door just as I am shutting the laptop. Luka runs to me and jumps in my lap. I can hear McKenna breathing heavily from where I am sitting.

"Hey stud, been home long?" she asks.

"About an hour or so."

"Oh, okay--you must have come in just after I

stepped out. We had fun outside, didn't we, Luka?" She asks, baby-talking the puppy. "I'm going to take a shower," she added. "I'm sweaty."

A week later, I receive a call from Goodwin. He tells me he has contacted the party about the wager and wants to talk to me in person. I leave the apartment and go to meet Goodwin. When I arrive at the house, he is in the Study with is head-deep in work, as usual.

"Reading anything good?" I ask.

"Research. . . How are you?"

"Well, I read the book. Learned a lot about my Origin."

"That's good. It'll help you connect. About the bet-- I spoke with my contacts, and they're willing to allow it."

"What are the odds?"

"You're a four-to-one underdog. With Ken's record and that katana, people are doubtful you'll win this time. There's a fifty-thousand minimum. Remember, I followed your progress before Legacy, so I know you can cover that. How much are you looking to put down?"

"Two-fifty."

"I wasn't expecting that much! You have something special planned?"

"No. Two hundred and fifty is a nice round number. Besides, I'm married now. I have to make sure McKenna is taken care of in case anything were ever to happen to me."

"So you're worried?"

"No. I just want to build up my bank balance. And I don't lose."

"Fair enough."

"Who's holding the bet?" I ask.

Goodwin grins. "I'd love to tell you, but I can't. Just win, and you'll quadruple your stake."

"I can't thank you enough. How does ten percent sound?"

"Keep your money. I told you, you're like one of my own. Anyway, I'm heading out of here--I'll walk out with you."

I walk Goodwin to his car. Just as we get to it, Lazarus Caius Crassus appears. The very sight of him enrages me to the point where I want to remove his head from his excessively cologned body. Goodwin could tell and whispers to me, "Whoa, calm down, killer. Let me handle this. Lazarus!" He calls out.

"Thomas. What a pleasant surprise. I wanted to speak with Shieldsie. Is he in?"

"No, not at the moment. Can I be of any help?"

"The Third Proelium is coming up, as you know. Higher powers have just informed me that there will be a substitution."

Goodwin seems instantly apprehensive. "Substitution? For whom?"

"It seems Nikko will no longer face off against the Khan fighter. The Assembly would like to see the battle of Troy played out again. Owen will be fighting in the undercard against Nikko just before the battle of the Echoes plays out. The Assembly probably feels that Legacy could profit greatly before the Final Proelium if all three active Echoes battle on the same night. Think of all the money that will be changing hands!"

"What did you do?" Goodwin demands.

"Thomas, I'm hurt. You know me better than that. Do you think I'm capable of arranging such a change?"

"Yes."

"Well," Lazarus chuckles, "so I am. That much is true. But this time, I had nothing to do with it. I met with the Assembly when they heard that Nikko's opponent had suffered a terrible training accident. His opponent is said to be unfit to fight. They proceeded to ask if my men are ready. Of course, I said yes--and I mentioned how much they would stand to profit if Owen and Nikko met each other in the arena. Achilles verse Hector again--a chance to rewrite history!"

Goodwin, distressed by the information, can't even look Lazarus in the eye. He combs his fingers through his hair.

"You are not going to get away with this," Goodwin says.

"Thomas, think of all the revenue. The battle of Troy will prove to be one of the greatest events in Legacy history. I'm sure Luke is itching to see this fight. Aren't you, son?" Lazarus asks me.

"Never call me that," I snap. "I am not your son."

"I know, boy, it's just a figure of speech. By the way, I saw your last fight. Simply delightful. I loved watching you cut off his hands. Full of surprises, aren't you?"

"That's funny, Lazarus. I heard you paid Erno to kill me. How did that one turn out for you?"

He snickers. "Kill you? Heavens, no--that was a misunderstanding. I simply placed a bet in favor of Erno to win. Say, I hear you got married. Congratulations. I'm sure your wife is a fine piece of work."

"Hold your tongue or lose it!"

"If I were you, I would keep her close to my side. Who knows? Someone might just sneak up and gain a position next to her. From what I hear--at least from Owen--she's easily swayed."

What was he trying to imply? This information isn't something I care to find out from him. I am about to kill him when Goodwin blocks my path. "If he wasn't standing between us right now," I growl, "I'd cut your heart out and feed it to my dog."

"Very good!" Lazarus exclaims. "Why, with such

passion, maybe we should speak about you fighting for me. That way, I wouldn't need to kill you. I can make it worth your while! How about it?"

"Go to hell!"

"Hell? Please, I've sent Orcus so much business; he owes me a favor."

"Lazarus," said Goodwin, "you are not welcome here. You'd best leave before he decides that my barrier isn't going to stop him anymore."

Lazarus shrugs blithely. "Fine, fine--but where's Nikko? Since Shields isn't here, I would like to deliver the message myself. I'd love to see his face when he finds out he gets a chance to honor the great Hector!"

I couldn't take it anymore. I move Goodwin out of the way and wrap my hands around Lazarus's throat tighter than the clutches of a lion's jaws. Lazarus struggles to free himself.

"Luke, not here! Not here!" Goodwin barks, prying my hand loose.

"Strong grip," Lazarus murmurs. "I'll be sure to remember that. Tell Nikko to be ready--come the Third Proelium, he will meet his end." Lazarus collects himself and saunters off. Before he is out of sight, Lazarus pauses in step, turns around, and adds, "Congratulations once again on your marriage."

I feel like he is hinting at something. I wish I were fighting Owen in Nikko's place. I'm sure he can beat Owen, but Owen is the fight I've been hunting.

I have to keep calm. My fight is just around the corner, and I need to focus my energy on Ken. I know McKenna wouldn't lie to me, but the way Lazarus mentioned that thing with Owen. I'm going to have to talk to her about it.

A week passes, and Shields is still missing. Goodwin is starting to grow concerned. He told me it was unlike Shields to be gone so long. The last time anyone had seen him was the night of the Second Proelium. We are a week away from the Third, and he is still nowhere to be found. Goodwin was forced to tell Nikko about the change in the bout. He'd hoped Shields would be the one to do so. Nikko deserved to know--and seemed to have taken the news pretty hard. He, too, had not been around Aurelius of late. I want to talk to him about the fight if I can.

Walking down the halls of Aurelius when I notice something out the corner of my eye: Shields' office door was cracked open. Was he there? I push the door open and peer in; there is no one in the office, but the entrance to the Arsenal is ajar. I head down to the room and see Shields standing inside. "You're alive!" I shout.

"Of course I'm alive--you think it's that easy to kill me?"

"Where have you been? No one's seen you since the last Proelium. Mr. Goodwin was starting to get worried."

"I was away on business. No big deal. I'm back now." Shields is acting as if he's been away for a day or so. I got the feeling he is hiding something.

"Did you hear Owen's going to fight Nikko in the Proelium?"

"Lazarus arranged the entire thing. Nikko doesn't want to fight Owen. Nikko knows he's good, but he can't beat Owen. Hector knew he wouldn't be able to defeat Achilles either. No matter who you are, your past can always haunt you. There are only two people in Legacy who can defeat Owen." He is referring to Ken and me--the only two other Echoes in Legacy, which is why Owen has never fought Ken. Lazarus didn't want to take the chance of Owen losing; he wants to protect his investment.

"If you haven't seen Nikko," Shields says, "it's most likely because he's home praying to Apollo to protect him in battle and saying goodbye. He probably never told you this because he is a very private individual, but Nikko has a wife and son."

"Owen's going to kill him if he gets the chance?"

"It's in his blood."

I didn't want to even think about that. Nikko is a great friend; I don't know how I would react if he dies. There has to be something we can do. "Let me take his place?"

"Unfortunately, Lazarus was able to strike a deal. Besides, it doesn't work like that. The Assembly doesn't change its mind on matches unless doing so will improve the Proelium. They're not going to give up reliving one of the greatest wars in history, plus a battle between Echoes so that you can fight Owen.

Anyhow, the fight hasn't taken place yet--we don't know for sure if Nikko will lose. History doesn't always have to repeat itself--that's why we teach it in classrooms so that people have the opportunity to not fall into the same patterns and habits of those before them. We can be better than before and not hindered by the past. Live for the future. Nikko is of Hector's blood, but he is his own person. Only he is the master of his fate."

"I will kill Lazarus," I swear.

"Don't worry about him. Lazarus is going to get what he has coming to him."

Shields sounds pretty confident in that statement. I know Shields won't hesitate to send Lazarus to the afterlife, considering what he's done to him.

The whole time we have been talking, Shields has been collecting weapons. So what is he doing with all that stuff? It's like he's arming himself for war.

"Is that an actual extension knife?" I ask about a weapon I notice sitting on the table.

"Yes. It was a gift from an old friend."

I have never seen one in real life, only in movies

and video games. Assassins would conceal them in their sleeves and deliver a deadly blow to their targets without them seeing it coming.

Shields looks hard at me. "Are you ready to face Ken?"

"Of course. Ken won't expect me to fight him with my weapons, which should give me the advantage. If I feel I'm losing control of the fight, though, I'll have to disarm him and fight him to my strength."

"Do not fight Ken forcefully. Let him advance on you and then react. You must be able to get close to him to defeat him. Fight from a distance, and you're no match for his katana."

With a sword just about four feet long, there is no way I can fight him from a distance. The closer I am to him, the harder it would be for him to use that blade on me. That's easier said than done.

Friday comes quickly, and in no time, we are on the eve of the Proelium. After training for the day, I go to the locker room to change and finally see Nikko. It is a relief for me. Nikko has been gone since the news broke to him about the Proelium.

I can't describe the expression on Nikko's face. It's as if someone has taken the light from the world, and he is living in the darkness. He is standing at his locker, looking at pictures.

"Nikko?" I say, trying to see if he will acknowledge me.

"You know, when I first fought in Legacy, I almost pissed my pants thinking about the possibility of death. Then, when I won and continued to win, I didn't get the sensation you would expect. Aurelius became my family, and I was honored to represent them as a member and as the Bloodborn of Hector. Now, I have that terrible feeling again about death. I almost forgot what it felt like."

"Owen is not Achilles. He's not a god! You can best him in the arena."

"I can best him in the arena. . .I'm no fool. I'm a good fighter, but that's where my abilities end. This fight is nothing more than a tribute to the Assembly to see if Hector could've indeed best Achilles, and I'm no better than Hector was. The gods have shown favor to Owen. He is special, whether I want to admit it or not. And, I am just a man."

"What about your family?" I ask, trying to light a fire in him.

"Shields told you, didn't he? I took this week to spend as much time with my wife and son as possible. She needs to be prepared if I...if I don't come back. I have prayed to Apollo to protect me in battle, and if he sees fit, he will answer my prayers. I have been blessed to find love and success thus far in my life. Now I have the opportunity to rewrite history. There are many things I would lay my life down for, and the honor of Aurelius is one of them!"

CHAPTER 9: THE THIRD PROELIUM

The energy of the crowd is different tonight. Usually, on Proelium nights, the crowd is full of energy, as if they are anxious to see a fight. But, tonight, there is a peculiar vibe--the people seem hungry. I can tell because the voices are swarming in a deranged, fanatic hush. They have come to see blood and to witness death.

There isn't an empty seat in the house. Security has been beefed up in anticipation of the Proelium. With all the high-priced suits and evening gowns filling in, I assume many important people have come to see a once-in-a-lifetime event, the rematch of Hector and Achilles--and, as a bonus, a battle of Echoes.

There are only two fights for this event which

means there is no time to mentally prepare. Shields said no one would care about the undercards. The Assembly would stand to profit more by focusing the Proelium solely on the main events. The crowd wouldn't have to wait to see what they've come for.

Not a single member of Aurelius has failed to attend. They have all traveled with us to the arena. There is no laughing, no music, no conversation-- only silence. We all know what's the stakes are. The intention isn't to be somber, but the fear of the unknown is heavily lurking.

The crowd is growing impatient. There's no more time to fear anticipation. The time has come for the gladiators to take the sand.

Nikko kneels to pray to the gods, as he always does before every fight. In his honor, the House of Aurelius joins in as well. When he has finished his prayers, Nikko rises and declares, "The Gods are with us tonight. If this night was supposed to be easy, we wouldn't be in this room. I am faced with a task that is bigger than me, bigger than my opponent. Tonight, I have the chance to rewrite history and bring glory to those men and women who died at the expense of an unnecessary war. We are cursed and blessed to bear the burden of being born of great bloodlines. We can't deny that this is what we live for. Aurelius has been my family since I first joined, and I shall honor you all in battle tonight. There are only two ways to become a legend--win the crowd and never lose! For the brotherhood!"

"For Aurelius!" We call out.

Nikko smiles and embraces us as a group. The brothers of Aurelius leave us for final preparations and go to take their seats amongst the people. Shields, Nikko, and I are the only ones left in the room.

"Give this to my wife," Nikko says as he hands Shields a note. "And Luke, give him hell tonight."

"You don't have to fight him," I say. "We can--"

"I appreciate the concern," he interjects, shaking his head. "I know that my reservations reveal my fears, but this is what I was born for. Owen is a man like any other--he bleeds like you and me. Tonight, he, too, will have to stand before me and, in the arena, where all men are equals."

Nikko picks up his sword, his shield and takes a breath. He walks towards the sand, pausing at the gate, waiting to be presented to the crowd.

"Welcome to the most anticipated Proelium in Legacy history!" The Master of Ceremonies roars in a deep, booming voice. "Delivered from the sands of time, the battle of the ages. I give to you Nikko, born of Hector, and Owen, the Echo of Achilles!"

The Sphere walls start vibrating from the screams of eager patrons as the crowd stands to their feet. Then, finally, the gates rise, and Nikko and Owen ascend from the darkness, never once breaking eye contact. I look up at the crowd and see Lazarus Crassus taking his seat in the solarium.

Nikko and Owen face off in the center of the arena, both eager to start. They take their positions and raise their weapons.

"Come to die?" Owen asks. I can hear everything from behind the gate.

"I was going to ask you the same thing!" Nikko replies.

Owen begins attacking, and Nikko defending

superbly. They seem to be evenly matched. Neither wants to be the first on the receiving end of a blade. Nikko led with his shield and follows up by landing a blow to Owen's chin with the pommel of his sword. Nikko is fighting like a man possessed. Usually, he fights by the book, never trying to look spectacular-- but tonight, he is performing like I'd never seen out of him. The crowd loves it, and Owen is feeling the heat.

Nikko lands several close shots. Owen is doing his best to deflect them, but Nikko is relentless.

Owen draws first blood when he strikes Nikko on the shoulder with his sword. Nikko is starting to have trouble raising his shield. However, he does his best to fight through, landing a strike to Owen's chest. The crowd reigns down praise as blood begins to rain all over the sand.

I can see Nikko favoring his arm, but he retakes the offensive. They lock up and start throwing punches at one another. Owen lands two clean shots to Nikko's face, dazing him for a second. Trying to recompose himself, Nikko sends another blow to Owens's face from the pommel of his sword and delivers an elbow to Owen's arm, causing him to drop his shield.

"Lets go!" I shout to Nikko. It's all I can do since I can't be out there with him. This is his fight, still, I know how much this means to him and how much he has riding on tonight.

Nikko is in a good position in the match, but the close-quarter combat is wearing heavily. The strength in his wounded arm is quickly failing. Nikko's shield has become too heavy to hold, and he is forced to drop his defensive weapon. Both fighters are battered and, as the minutes pass, they are breathing more and more heavily.

The crowd knows they are witnessing an epic battle--Hector and Achilles reborn in the rematch of the century. I glance at the audience again. Linc, Juliet, McKenna, and Bobby are sitting with the brothers of Aurelius, yelling at the top of their lungs. I catch another glimpse of Lazarus at the edge of his seat, realizing that Nikko isn't going to lie down and die.

They engage in close-quarter combat once again. Owen lands a two-move combo, hitting Nikko in the face and quickly slashing him across the chest. It pains me to watch the blood burst from my friend's body.

Nikko retreats, trying to gather himself. He looks around Owen, and we lock eyes briefly. The look he gives me will haunt my mind eternally.

Nikko continues to battle through the pain. Knowing that he has Nikko where he wants him, Owen comes after him again. Nikko avoids the advance, rolling out of the attack and cutting Owen on the heel. Exhaustion is now set in on both of the fighters. Owen drops to one knee after enduring Nikko's last successful strike.

The crowd is euphoric--non-stop mayhem in the Sphere as Nikko and Owen have collided on the sand.

After a quick breath, Owen rises to his feet. Nikko is shocked by Owen's stamina. He can't believe Owen is getting up after the damage inflicted to his leg. With no intention of quitting, Nikko squares off to face him. It is as if the man hadn't even been affected by his Achilles tendon being severed. Owen advances and swings his sword. Nikko deflects it with the shield he has once again picked up. The force of the blow sends Nikko backward, though, onto the ground. Wasting no time, Owen moves in. Nikko tries to frantically escape, but Owen isn't letting up.

It is obvious Nikko has nothing left in him. Owen steps back just for a moment, long enough that Nikko can get to his knees and concede. The fight is over just like that--but just as Nikko hangs his head, Owen shoves his weapon through Nikko's chest. The tip of the sword is painted in blood as it comes out of his back. Owen removes the sword from Nikko's chest, and thirty thousand screaming people watch as Nikko's body falls limp and he crashes forward to the sand.

The House of Aurelius rushes the pitch after Nikko's murderer, and the members of Crassus meet them in his defense. A brawl ensues before security can step in to mute the scuffle. Shields runs onto the sand to tend to Nikko. There is no movement; he is unresponsive as the blood drains out of his wound and saturates the sand.

"Get him up," Shields demands, telling the brothers

to carry Nikko's body back to the barracks.

As the sea of people cleared the floor, Owen and I stood staring one another down, unblinking. He knows what I am thinking, and I made sure nothing gets lost in translation.

In the locker room, everyone is enraged and distraught over the death of their leader. Talk of killing Owen, of retaliation against Crassus, has already begun, and I share the group's feelings. Owen will pay for what he's done.

"Listen to me!" I demand. "Nikko's death will be avenged, but now is not the time. If he was able to wake, he would tell you the same. Grieve for his family, and mourn for your brother, who has just perished in battle. He gave his all in that arena for you. Honor him, and worry about Crassus later."

The crowd is still amped after the first fight. I don't have time to allow sorrow to set in. Those people demand more blood, and the Master of Ceremonies has already begun to announce the next fight.

"Luke, stay focused," Shields tells me as I head back to the arena.

"The battle of Echoes is underway! Tonight, two of the greatest fighters Legacy has ever seen square off in battle. I present to you the man who has captured all your hearts. From Aurelius, Luke, the Echo of Spartacus!"

The gate opens, and I enter the arena. The cheers for me grow louder every time I take a step. I can't help but notice even more people are wearing the red ribbon in my honor. I find McKenna in the crowd; she mouths the words I love you to me. I wink back. Nikko's death is still fresh on my mind, but I have to focus on Ken.

"Now," the deep voice calls out, "the Echo of the greatest swordsman the world has ever seen. The demon has once again returned to the Sphere. From Khan, Ken Musashi, the Echo of Miyamoto Musashi."

As Ken comes out of the entrance, it's my first time seeing him. He has an athletic build, long black hair just past his shoulder, and is average height. Ken is wearing black pants. His katana is fastened to his hip and has no armor whatsoever. The most noticeable thing is the striking mask he is wearing-- a dark red samurai men-yoroi, in the form of a fierce-looking demon, the only visible part of his face his eyes and brows, which are perched right above the top of the mask.

Ken dips his head to me as a sign of respect, and I do the same. As soon as we come out of bows, the fight is on. I can immediately tell he is calculating. We circle each other for a moment, neither wanting to make the first move. Finally, Ken unsheaths his sword with lightning speed and attacks. I deflect two quick assaults before he comes at me again. I stick to the game plan by staying on the defensive and waiting for my opportunity. I am doing my best to deflect and avoid his flurry of attempts. Ken counters with a kick to my thigh, and I land a right cross to his face. He swings the katana, just missing my head, and I counter with a push-kick to his abdomen, the force of which makes him stumble. Ken regains his balance and charges at me. He is too fast and good with the katana. I am struggling against the storm of attacks he keeps throwing my way. The sword is so sharp. I am soon bleeding from both of my arms, though I hadn't felt the blows.

I had a feeling that was going to happen. I wasn't going to beat Ken fighting him weapon to weapon. We advance at the same time. Our weapons get hooked in a stalemate. Neither of us will back down. We are Both doing our best to overpower the other. Finally, Ken and I break out of the lock but drop our weapons as we do. It is my time to strike.

He is better than I expect in hand-to-hand combat. He is keeping up for a while, but I am too much for him to handle. I land a two-punch combo followed by a head kick that puts him down. Ken races for his sword, but I am already standing over him with my falcata trained on his neck. He knows he has nowhere to go. Ken does the honorable thing and chooses to concede. The crowd is begging for his death, but I extend my hand to Ken and help him to his feet.

"That was a great fight, Luke," he says.

"Thanks, man. You. too."

"Good luck in the next Proelium," he offers as he heads back towards his barracks.

I am relieved to have won, but it comes at a bittersweet time. In the locker room, Nikko's body lay on a table, wrapped in a bloodstained sheet. His shield, and the sword of Troy, lay beside him.

"What will become of his body?" I ask Shields.

"He will be taken back to Aurelius. Arrangements have been made. Nikko will meet the afterlife with a burial fit for a king."

I get cleaned up and meet McKenna and the others in the parking lot. We drive to Aurelius, no time wasted in sending Nikko home. There are hundreds of people gathered behind the house when we arrive. Torches are burning high all around the yard. Everyone has congregated around a massive wooden altar that has been constructed for Nikko. His body, stiff and still wrapped in cloth, is lying on a bed of flowers above this pyre. The only visible part of him is his uncovered head.

Shields approaches a woman standing in the front of the crowd adjacent to us and presents her with Nikko's sword and shield. I assume she is Nikko's wife.

After briefly speaking to the woman, Shields

climbs to the top of the burial structure and stands before the body. He places a gold coin on both of Nikko's eyelids--payment to the ferryman.

"This is an unpleasant night. For we have been stripped of our beloved, friend, and brother. Nikko was a leader in every sense of the word. He drove us to greatness beyond our knowledge and was loyal without bounds. He honored his family and Origin till his end. Nikko is survived by his wife and son." Shields picks up a torch beside the pyre.

"Rest in peace," he says as he touches the fire to the wood, igniting the structure. We watch as the flames engulf Nikko's body. The heat is blistering; the fire burns brightly until the burial mound is reduced to rubble and ash.

The crowd slowly disperses. McKenna and I stay until everyone is gone. Goodwin approaches me. "I know this is a bad time, but I have something for you," he says. We follow him to his office.

"I didn't want to give this to you outside." Goodwin hands me a black bag. "Your winnings. The people who took the bet are interested in finding out if you'd like to work with them again."

"Probably. We'll have to wait till the next Proelium to find out."

McKenna and I leave Aurelius feeling drained. When we walk through the front door, Luka is there to greet us. He is getting so big.

Even while lying in bed, I can't stop thinking about Nikko. I can't stop thinking about his family.

It makes me think about McKenna. What would happen to her if she lost me? How would I fare if anything ever happened to her? The thought weighs heavily on me. McKenna comes to bed and lays her head on my chest; the smell of her hair comforts me.

Aurelius is empty the next day. Everyone, I guess, has taken time to mourn. I decided to stop in to see if Goodwin was around. When I get to the Study, Shields is in with him.

"Luke, glad you're here," Goodwin says. "We need to talk. Sources tell us that Nikko wasn't supposed to make it out of the Proelium alive. The Assembly had ordered his death. He would've had to kill Owen to survive."

"The Assembly ordered him dead?" I can't believe it. "What can we do about this?"

"Nothing, once they make a decision."

Shields doesn't say much. He is just quiet the whole time. All is he is doing is leaning against the wall, staring at the floor.

"Professor Shields? What do you suggest?" I ask.

"Nothing. The Assembly is still in power--for now. These are the laws of Legacy. Set your sight to the final Proelium. Right now, I have to go. I have business to see to."

"What's up with him?" I ask Goodwin.

"Don't worry about Shields. He's just angry, like everyone else. He's right, though-- Nikko is gone, and we can't change that."

I don't want to just let it go. I don't care if it is the law of Legacy either. As far as I am concerned, Owen murdered Nikko, and I won't let that go unavenged.

"It's also been brought to our attention," Goodwin goes on, "that Lazarus may have an affiliation with the Assembly. At this point, we don't know to what extent, but our sources tell us his ties may run deep. If this is true, then the corruption of Legacy may be past cleansing."

CHAPTER 10: TRAGEDY STRIKES AURELIUS

Training, as usual, picks back up at Aurelius. Three weeks have passed since Nikko's death. We are still feeling the effects but are starting to deal with them. Goodwin is once again in charge of the house--Shields still has not returned.

I don't stay long at Aurelius. McKenna and I haven't done anything together for a while. So I thought it would be good for us to get out for a night on the town. I take her back to Soleil, the restaurant we had gone to for our anniversary. After that night, it had become one of her favorite restaurants. I figured she would appreciate a date there.

"This place is more beautiful every time we come,"

she remarks.

"I'm glad. Only the best for my wife."

"...I still can't believe Nikko is gone. He conceded, and Owen still took his life. Isn't there anything that can be done?"

"Unfortunately, no. Owen's time is coming."

"Who was that girl Shields gave Nikko's sword to?"

"Nikko's wife. Shields told me the day before the Proelium that Nikko was, in fact, married and had a son."

McKenna is taken aback. "Is rivalry worth a man's life? Nikko's wife and son shouldn't have to suffer because of something neither of them had anything to do with."

She is right.

"Do you worry about me fighting?" I ask.

Before I started in Legacy, I had asked McKenna if she would be okay with it, and she'd said yes. Since I'd been in it, though, I had never asked her again.

"To be honest with you, I can't sit here and tell you I sleep like a baby. The reality of death and severe injury are more real once you're actually exposed to them. It's weird to think that the nights before every Proelium, I dream of you in battle. I see you fighting and always have dreams of vivid outcomes. The fighting is exciting, but I'm scared for you more and more each time. You'd think, with your success, the fear would subside, but it doesn't. I don't know how Nikko's wife could do it, to let Nikko fight and not watch him in battle. I refuse for you to be out of my sight. As long as you fight, I will be there to watch. I will not get a call saying you will not be coming home to me that night."

"You want to know something interesting?"

"What?"

"One day, Goodwin lent me a book that had information on Spartacus, everything about him, birth to death and in between. After reading it cover to cover, I'd learned about his wife. History tells us that he was married and that his wife was a prophetess. She too could see visions of her husband."

McKenna seems comforted by that. I guess, in a way, it gave her more of a connection to me.

The night goes beautifully. We enjoyed the

restaurant, and nothing could've ruined this night--or so I thought. Then I get a call from Bobby.

"Hey, what's--"

"Luke, come quick! I don't know what to do! He won't respond."

"Bobby, what are you talking about? Where are you?"

"My--my dad! My dad's been stabbed. He's losing a lot of blood. Please, you have to come now. We're at Aurelius."

I tell McKenna what is going on. We immediately get up and race to the car. The drive feels like it's taking hours. Bobby flags us down when we arrive. He is kneeling over his father, lying in Bobby's arms, and pressing his shirt against his father's wound. Goodwin has lost a lot of blood and is starting to turn cold. We load him into my car and rush to the hospital.

Outside of the emergency room, Bobby gets the attention of two nurses who appear to be on break. They grab a nearby gurney and cart Goodwin immediately into a trauma bay. Bobby is a wreck.

"Bobby, listen to me. What happened?"

"I don't know. My dad, Kanae, and I went to dinner together. They hadn't met yet, and I really wanted him to get to know her. Everything was going great. We rode together to the restaurant, so on the way back, we stop by Aurelius. Dad said he'd left something important in the Study. As he was walking inside, out of nowhere, these guys jumped him. Kanae and I were in the car when it started. We raced out to come to his aid, fending them off, and...and that's when I called you. I panicked--I saw the blood, and I didn't know who else to call."

"Don't worry about it, man. Where's Kanae?" I ask, wondering why she isn't with us.

"I don't know. Kanae disappeared after those bastards ran off. All she said was please not to tell anyone."

"About what?"

"Kanae is the one who fought the guys off, Luke. Honestly, she fought like you. These guys were twice her size, with short blades, and she destroyed them. I wanted to thank her, but I didn't know where she'd gone."

We wait in the lobby for hours while the doctors worked on Goodwin. Finally, one of them came out and told us that he was in critical but stable condition. Bobby went in to see him.

We stay for a couple more hours before we have to go home. McKenna needs some rest. I can't have her sleeping in a hospital lobby, worrying all night.

I can't sleep myself, wondering whether or not Goodwin would pull through. Who would want to hurt him? My thoughts point directly to Lazarus. He seems to be spending most of his time plotting against Aurelius and me. I know in my gut that he has something to do with it.

And why had Kanae run off? Why hadn't she wanted Bobby to tell anybody about what she'd done? She's a nice girl, but is she Lazarus's spy, sent to infiltrate our group?

I don't want to jump to conclusions, but I need to speak to her.

The next day I wait in the quad for Kanae to appear. To my luck, she does. I hop off the bench I am sitting on and approach her. She doesn't notice me coming, so I surprise her when I tap her on the shoulder.

"What's up?" I ask.

"Oh, Luke! You startled me."

"Have you, spoken to Bobby recently?"

"Yeah, I did this morning. I heard Mr. Goodwin is in the hospital. It's so sad."

"Cut the act. I know you were there last night. What I don't know is, why did you run off?"

"That's none of your business." Angered, she tries to leave.

"So you did have something to do with Bobby's father stabbing!" I yell. People turn and look at us because of the scene I've just caused. Kanae stops in her tracks and comes back toward me.

"You don't know what you're talking about," she says, biting off each word.

"Answer my question." She looks around to make sure no one is listening. I can tell she is dreading answering the question.

"I had nothing to do with those guys. I didn't know who they were. I ran off because no one can find out who I am. It was already too much for Bobby to handle, seeing his dad bleeding like that. He didn't need to know about me, too. When he called you, I knew you'd come, so he was in good hands. I ended the attack, so he'd be okay until you got there."

It still isn't making sense to me. Why would it be an issue for anyone to know who Kanae is and about her fighting ability? I take a step closer.

"Why isn't anyone allowed to know you can fight?" I whisper.

"You don't know my family, Luke. They have expectations of me. I can be almost anything I want--a doctor, lawyer, music virtuoso--but fighting is strictly prohibited. If my parents were to find out I got into another altercation, they'd have my head."

"Another?"

She sighs, looks down at the ground, and back up at me. She met my eyes with a flat, gunner's gaze. "I am the Echo of Tomoe Gozen, the Onna-bugeshia. A female Samurai, you'd say. She was a beautiful warrior who fought and survived the Genpei War. I came into my abilities at an early age and ran into a lot of trouble because of it. My parents are afraid that if people knew

I am an Echo, it would put my life in danger. They won't let me get sucked into the world of Legacy.

"I, I really do love Bobby, and I know it was wrong for me to leave him there. I will tell him the truth, but on my own time."

"Why--"

"Look, Luke. I'm sorry, but I can't talk anymore. I have to go."

An Echo? Of all the things about the world of Legacy that I knew, a female Echo was not among them. Still, of all the girls in the world, Bobby had fallen for the perfect one for him.

I drive back over to the hospital. Bobby is still there; he hasn't left his father's side since we first arrived. Goodwin has been moved to a private room. When I got there, Bobby is sitting in a chair next to the bed. He looks terrible, his face gloomy and pale. He is staring out the window at the overcast sky.

"Do you believe in Heaven, Luke?" he asks as I walked in.

"Heaven? I guess I've never really given much thought to the matter, but I suppose I do. I mean, if there is a divine transcendent paradise where we spend our afterlife, I would hope that those I love would be transported there when their time comes."

"My father believes. Being a Historian, he's studied a lot of different societies and cultures. He'd say there is one common belief among them that was irrefutable--the divine creation and an afterworld. He said that to deny the existence of a god or the heavens would be to accuse all of mankind of being a sham. And he said...he said that, when his time came, he hopes that he'll be able to look down on me from up there and rejoice, and be proud of the man I have become. What I'm trying to say is, the doctor told me he's dying. The knife lacerated vital organs that are too fragile to operate on. They made him as comfortable as possible, but he has two days at most."

I am speechless. "I'm sorry, Bobby."

"You should say goodbye. He'll be up soon. I know he'd want to speak with you before he goes." Bobby tells me.

"I ran into Kanae today. She said she is sorry. After everything that went down last night, she didn't know how to handle it. You should call her. You need to talk to her."

"I guess...I need to take a walk." He gets out of his chair, straightens his clothes, and disappears down the hall.

It is weird sitting there by myself. The silence is menacing. The only noise in the room is from the heart monitor and muffled announcements coming through the heavy wooden hospital door. I gaze at Goodwin in admiration. The doctors had done their best to stop the bleeding, but I could see traces of red seeping through the bandages. I didn't know what to say.

I can't help but feel it is too early for him to go. He's been through a lot, but there is still much he needed to see. The day his son walks his bride down the aisle, to the birth of his first grandchild. What is Bobby supposed to do now?

Goodwin starts moving his head and blinking. He is waking up.

"How are you feeling?" I ask.

"Luke. Thanks for coming. I'm in a lot of pain, but

the doctors are doing their best to keep me at ease."

"Bobby hasn't slept since we brought you in here."

"This is hard for him to handle. I can't leave him now. I knew one day I would pass away, and he would have to bury me, but it wasn't supposed to happen like this. I was supposed to get old, and he was going to send me off when he had a family of his own to take care of."

Goodwin breathes out slowly and breathes in again. "When I'm gone, he's going to need you, Luke. You're his best friend. He thinks of you as a brother. For a long time, it was just Bobby and me. I never told him the truth about his mother. He thinks she passed away when he was a baby, but that's not what happened. I came home one night to find the house empty and my wife nowhere to be found. I could hear Bobby crying in the nursery. He'd been left alone, unattended.

"I was furious, but the worst thoughts were going through my head. What happened to her? Did someone break in and abduct her? That was the only reason I could think of why she would be missing. I picked Bobby up out of the bassinet. He was only an infant. I was heading for the phone when I found the note. She'd left it on the table in the hallway. In big letters on the front it said READ THIS. . . . I will never forget the words:

Thomas,

You could not begin to fathom how unhappy I am living in this house. The only time I find joy is when you and that kid are not around. Do not look for me! I am not in danger. For some time now, I have kept up a relationship with a man that I am genuinely in love with, someone who isn't you. When the time comes to explain to Bobby why I am not in his life, tell him I died. It should be easier than telling him the truth. Even he shouldn't have to know that I can't have anything to do with either of you. Good luck.

I wish things could've been different...

"I've never had the heart to tell him what really happened. That note left me sick to my stomach. I wanted to die at first. I never could get over what she had done to us. I obsessed over her words until I realized that she lied. There was no other man. His mother had just left. We were so happy up until that day, then out of the blue, she was gone. I used to call her my deadly flower. There was always something dangerous about her that attracted me to her. But, the pain of that night is why I never remarried. It was hard to deal with, but watching Bobby grow up over the years has made me forget about her."

There is a knock at the door. It's Goodwin's nurse; she's come to change his bandages. She told me that he needed his rest and that it would be best to go home and get some myself.

"I'll be back," I promise Goodwin. He musters a smile and nods.

Before I leave, I look around for Bobby. He isn't anywhere in the building.

I drive back to the apartment. When I got there, McKenna is baking in the kitchen.

"How's Mr. Goodwin?"

"Dying." Just hearing myself say it out loud makes

me cringe. "The wound caused extensive internal damage. They can't operate on him. He's slowly bleeding to death."

The news leaves her silent. She wraps her arms around me.

"Do they know who did it?" McKenna asks.

"From what I was told, neither Bobby nor Kanae knew who the attackers were. I didn't ask Goodwin himself, but I have my suspicions about who's behind all of it--Lazarus Crassus, that sick bastard... There is only one person I truly need to talk to right now. I just hope he isn't away on business."

Morale at Aurelius is at an all-time low. Fragile spirits darken the halls and doorways of the house. The brothers all feel helpless. It's the second time in weeks that one of their own has been attacked. Something needs to be done.

I went to Shields' office and found, to my luck, that he is in. The room is, however, in disarray, and he in a rage. There is no one reason he shouldn't have been. Goodwin has been his best friend.

I can tell he has been thinking of something. There is only one chair in the office that hadn't been turned over. I pick the coat rack up off the floor and hung up the black-hooded cloak he has draped over the chair before I sit down. Shields has always been calm and cool-headed. It's a surprise to see his office in this condition.

"I take it you heard," I said.

"It wasn't a random mugging. Lazarus sent the men who attacked Goodwin. He is threatened by this house and wants it to fall."

I agree. But why Goodwin? What threat does he pose to Lazarus? I ask.

"For years now, Lazarus has been trying in various ways to get Thomas to come to Crassus. He was unsuccessful every time. Thomas is--was--the greatest Historian in Legacy, and Lazarus knew it. The Historian's job is to find bloodlines and seek out new fighters. This you know. The stronger the warriors, the more control and power you have. Lazarus was hell-bent on gaining high status in Legacy. That arrogance and egotism have been passed down in

Crassus's blood for ages. The man wants to mark his place in history and outdo his ancestor, credited with vanquishing Spartacus.

"Anyhow," Shields adds, slumping into the chair behind his desk, "Lazarus has theories about where he can find more Echoes. He wants to create what he calls a 'superior legion.' The first and only Echo in his house is Owen--the Echo of the greatest fighter the world has ever known. He's supposed to lead this undefeatable army of warriors." Shields sighs, and I can hear his anguish in it. "The only person who could have helped Lazarus realize this dream was Thomas. No other Historian has as an extensive command of the materials. Thomas used every bit of information possible to create what you know as the Study.

"But Lazarus is smarter than he may appear. Crassus has no chance of achieving a dominant position in Legacy as long as Thomas and the warriors of Aurelius endure. He will do everything in his power to take this house down brick by brick if given a chance. Thomas and Nikko were the cornerstones."

"We cannot let that happen!" I exclaim. "I will

march on them right now and take their lives if you tell me to!"

He is already shaking his head. "No, no. I have arranged a meeting with Lazarus. He gets away with this nonsense because I suspect he holds a seat on the Assembly council. To merely march on the house and start a war would be suicide. The Assembly will have our heads. The only way to defeat Lazarus is to give him what he most wants. I will have you fight Owen in the final Proelium. . .and I will be counting on you to take care of business, Luke. Owen must not leave the arena alive."

It was exactly what I had been waiting for. ". . .And Lazarus?"

"Leave Lazarus to me. I have other arrangements for him. I'll be meeting him at the Sphere. At eleven tonight, I want you to bring Linc and Taylor with you to accompany me. Given our colored history, I'm sure Lazarus will not be alone."

I head back to the hospital, calling them en route to let them know Shields's plan. They both said they'd be there, ready to act in case anything gets out of hand.

The hospital is busy and chaotic--there's always depressing energy in such places, so many sick and injured people; I feel uncomfortable spending so much time here.

Bobby is sitting outside the room, his body language, I notice, more at ease.

"What's going on?" I ask. "Anything new?"

"He's resting now. Earlier, his heart rate started to spike, but the doctors have it under control now. I saw Kanae earlier today."

"How was that?"

"She apologized for leaving so abruptly. She said she'd panicked after she fought off the attackers. She brought Dad flowers. I forgave her for the other night and thanked her. If it hadn't been for her, he'd already been dead, and me with him."

"Good. I'm happy for you."

"There is one thing, though. When I asked Kanae where she learned to fight like that, she couldn't tell me but that she would when the time is right. What do you think of that?"

I had no answer for him other than, "Don't worry

about that. If Kanae said she'd tell her truth, then allow her the time to do that."

We sit outside that hospital room for an hour before we go back in. Goodwin is awake but looks exhausted. "Dad, how are you?" Bobby asks.

"Hanging in there. Luke, you're back--it's good to see you."

"Good to see you too, sir. I spoke with Shields today. Have you had word from him?"

"Not yet. I'm sure he'll find his way here, though. He say anything?"

"Lazarus sent the men who attacked you." It came, clearly, as no surprise.

"Shields has arranged a meeting with him tonight at the Sphere. He's going to strike a deal for Owen and me to face each other in the final Proelium."

Bobby doesn't think that is a good idea by any means. "What?" Bobby declares. "Tell me you're not serious! Lazarus Crassus is not that easy to eliminate. Let's say for argument's sake that you are somehow able to defeat Owen. Then what? The man is the Echo of a demigod. Besides, even if he's killed, Lazarus will not quit!"

"It's the only way," said Goodwin. "Shields is right-- Lazarus can only be defeated by making him vulnerable before a strike. He has too many resources at his hand, mainly in the Assembly. This is a well-thought-out plan. Lazarus will be at his weakest with Owen out of the picture."

Bobby isn't so sure. "And what about McKenna? What about your wife? What is she going to do if you manage to get yourself killed?"

"If I do nothing," I told him flatly, "McKenna is already dead or widowed. As long as I am still living proof that Marcus Licinius Crassus did not end Spartacus's bloodline, Lazarus won't quit." I rest my hand on his shoulder. "Listen to me. I see the lengths this man will go to. You asked me what McKenna would do if I died. What will I do if I can no longer feel the warmth of her touch or hear the sound of her voice? What am I to do if her life is taken for the sake of the House of Crassus? Lazarus will come for me by any means he thinks best, but I will not allow my wife to be his first victim. No man who threatens the well-being of my wife will remain breathing, do you understand? If they try anything, I will cut off their heads and bathe in their blood."

"What time is the meeting tonight?" Goodwin asks.

"Eleven. Shields will be accompanied by Lincoln, Taylor, and me."

"Tell him to come by here afterward. There's not much time, and I need to speak with him. . . Bobby, I want to say this to you now. It's is time for you to assume the mantle as Historian of Aurelius. I wish it could've been under different circumstances, but you're ready. You have been for a long time."

Goodwin takes a deep breath and clears his throat. "After your mother died, it was you and me for the longest time. We had no other blood family, but we had each other. When I'm gone, I beg of you, don't think you're alone. Luke is your family now--your best friend, your brother. You are loved by many people. Never lose sight of that." Goodwin's words draw tears from Bobby's eyes. He sits beside the bed, grabbing his father's hand, and places his head against Goodwin's leg.

I sit with them for a while before I have to go to pick up the others. I give Goodwin a hug and tell him goodbye before I depart.

Linc is ready and waiting when I arrive. He wastes no time getting into the car. Taylor is at the house with Shields, who anticipated no hostilities; we would be there only to negotiate.

We arrive half an hour early. The Sphere is neutral ground, but Shields wants to scout ahead to ensure we aren't walking into an ambush.

At eleven on the dot, Lazarus strolls into the Sphere. And, as Shields had assumed, he is not alone. Owen and another Crassus goon are at his heels.

"Let me handle this," Shields whispers through clenched teeth. "Lazarus."

"Shieldsie, what a marvelous surprise! When you called me, I nearly leaped with excitement. But, then, I said to myself, I wonder what he wants to talk with me about?" Lazarus is smiling as he speaks.

"How come you brought them along?" Shields asks.

"To be honest, I wasn't sure if you were over the whole me- trying-to-kill-you thing. That was ages ago, but just in case you still had a thorn in your side about it--in our case, it was actually a knife--these young men came to make sure you didn't return the favor. And it appears you didn't travel alone either. Come now--don't you trust me?"

"I'd much rather trust a five-year-old with a handgun," Shields responds. "They too are here to make sure you didn't get any bright ideas. We need to talk about why I asked you down here."

"So formal. But I like it. Please, continue."

"I want to ask a favor of you."

"Favor? You are full of surprises tonight. How can I help?"

"You have some pull in the Assembly," Shields says. "For the final Proelium, Aurelius would like to challenge Crassus in the arena. For the main event, Aurelius offers Luke as the challenger against Owen."

"Really?" Lazarus asks, almost surprised. "You would see the Champion of Legacy paired against Owen? Are you not concerned about the possibility of him getting hurt? Or worse?"

"Minor concern. Aurelius offers this match as a

tribute to the Assembly. Luke is willing to die for the glory and honor of Legacy. How will he be given a chance at a glorious death if he does not face a true test in the arena?"

From the look on Lazarus's face, I can tell he is about to bite.

"It will be an honor to face Aurelius in the arena," he says. "I accept. To make things more interesting, however, why don't we make some alterations to the undercard?"

"What do you mean?"

"At the moment, we only honor the Assembly with a single fight. Though it will prove to be a great battle, the likes of which Legacy has never seen before, I think the Assembly deserves more praise than just the one bout." Shields doesn't like where this heading. "Say three more? Two one-on-one battles between fighters of our choosing, and, just before the main event, a battle royal among the best five fighters Aurelius has to offer and our five best--excluding Luke and Owen, of course!"

Shields ponders this itinerary for a moment. I

know he wants to turn it down. I was the only one who was supposed to fight in the Proelium--one battle to end Owen and set things in motion against Lazarus. There have been way too many people who have been affected already. Shields is trying to avoid putting anyone else in harm's way. He looks at me over his shoulder to glimpse my reaction.

"Cold feet, Shieldsie?" Lazarus asks.

"All right, don't get your panties in a bunch. I accept your terms."

"Brilliant. I can't wait for this spectacle. I really cannot wait!" Lazarus repeats. "In fact, I'm not going to. Three days from today, the final Proelium will take place."

Shields turns to leave.

"Tell your woman it was nice seeing her," Owen shouts at me.

Shields stops me before I can react.

"Speak about my wife again," I snap, "and no man will be able to stop me from causing you a slow and painful death."

"Whoa, save the passion for the arena!" Lazarus

chortles. "Shields, control your dog before I slap him on the bottom."

I broke free of Shields' grip on me, but his eyes tell me to cool off.

"Goodwin wants to see you when you leave here," I tell Shields.

I will wait for the Proelium. But, first, I need to talk to McKenna about what Owen has just said to me.

I don't wait for Linc, who rode with me to the Sphere. He'll have to find his own way home. I am pissed, and the only thing that matters right now is finding out the truth.

I try to calm myself before entering the apartment, but my suspicions are raging in my mind. McKenna and Luka are sitting on the couch, watching TV. McKenna glances at me and can tell something is wrong. She turns off the TV and looks at me, waiting for me to say what's on my mind. "I'm going to ask you a simple question, and I want you to tell me the truth," McKenna looks at me anxiously. "Did you and Owen see each other?"

Her head drops to her chest. "Yes, but it's not what

you think. I-I'm sorry I didn't tell you sooner. I didn't want you to find out like this."

Before she can say another word, I walk out. I need time to think and am too angry to have a successful conversation. I decide to get back in the car and drive for hours until the sun comes up.

In the morning, I get a call from Bobby. Goodwin has passed away in his sleep. I pull over on the side of the road. The news is hard to take, though I had known it was coming. I sit on the hood of my car for a while, reflecting.

I never would have imagined so much pain could come from this new life. I felt alone and taunted with loss at every turn. The thought of McKenna with Owen, and the news of Goodwin's passing, sent me to a dark place. I want to know the truth but am in no condition to listen. I will focus my energy instead on the Proelium, which's now days away. I am going to lock myself in the Arsenal, training until it's time to fight.

My phone starts to ring again. It's Bobby.

"What's up?" I ask when I answer.

"Luke, we need to talk. Where are you?"

"I don't know, but I'm on my way to Aurelius."

"Meet me there. I'll be in the Study."

I turn on my phone's GPS. To my surprise, I am only an hour away. I find my way back to Aurelius and go to the Study as soon as I enter the building. Bobby is inside with Kanae.

"Glad you got here so soon," he says. Shields came by the hospital last night and explained to my father what went down at the Sphere. Since the Proelium is only three days away, we have little time to waste. Owen is not an easy opponent, and you will need help if you are to defeat him. I was explaining the situation to Kanae, and she says she can assist."

I don't know if I should be offended by Bobby's lack of confidence in me, but I am open to hearing them out.

"I told you I would tell you on my own time, Bobby, what happened with me the other night," Kanae began. "If I'm going to adequately help, you'll need to know the truth about me. I am the Echo of Tomoe Gozen."

Bobby is predictably astonished. "Wait--so you're telling me you're an Echo?"

"Yes, I am."

"This is absolutely crazy!" Bobby exclaims. "Female Echoes are like myths in Legacy. There was a rumor once that one of the Assembly members is a female who happens to be the Echo of the Amazonian queen Penthesilea, who had fought for Troy... Why would you hide this?"

"Because of what you just said. There aren't any female Echoes in Legacy, and my parents wanted to protect me from this world. But I can no longer deny my Origin. I can't sit back and watch this fight I am a part of. But, right now, you need to forget that detail and pay attention to what I'm about to tell you. Since we've been dating, there are few things I've kept hidden from you. One, in particular, is my full name-- Kanae Akemi Musashi. Ken Musashi is my brother."

"Sibling Echoes?" Bobby's mind is blown. It's as if he just found the Holy Grail.

"Owen is a formidable opponent," she says. "He is skilled with both hand and sword. He has all the attributes of Achilles and none of his weaknesses. Case and point, when he wasn't affected by Nikko severing that tendon." She'd made a valid point. "So, to defeat him, you will need to best him with both hand and sword. Since my brother is the greatest swordsman in Legacy, I've asked him for a favor. You are the only fighter who has ever defeated him in the arena. He praises you as a worthy opponent. I asked him if he would train you for the fight. He said it would be an honor, and he's ready to start when you give the word."

I appreciated this. Ken is a great fighter--some could even argue I had been lucky to have beaten him. I happily accept his help and plan on starting immediately.

I thanked Kanae and got her brother's number so I can reach out to him. I immediately called Ken, and he agrees to meet at Aurelius. I leave Bobby and Kanae in the Study to work out their future. I know I should probably do the same with McKenna, but I am still not ready to speak. I haven't been home since I confronted her. This silence can't go on forever, and I am not going to allow it to. But I need time to collect my thoughts.

Ken arrives at Aurelius, and Kanae introduces Bobby and me before we begin.

The next couple of days are a blur. I live in Aurelius, sharpening my sword skills. With Ken's help, I've improved tenfold in forty-eight hours. And, the day before the Proelium, Ken's training is complete. He and I have formed a strong bond over these last two days.

"You're a fast learner," he says. "Owen, better have prepared for the fight of his life tomorrow, or he'll find himself on the wrong side of your blade."

"Thank you for training me. You're a fierce opponent, but above all, I now have the privilege of calling you a friend."

"Thanks--coming from you, that means a lot. I never faced anyone in the arena that could beat me, but you did. If there's anyone who can defeat Owen, it's you. I'll be watching you tomorrow, fight with honor."

McKenna and I have not spoken in two days, and I

miss her. I am ready to know what really happened, and I am prepared to listen. I race home, hoping to catch her before she goes to sleep.

When I got there, the apartment is silent. Luka is excited to see me and greets me as I walk in. He is getting so big and isn't even a year yet-- he's at least a hundred pounds and looks like a wolf.

I call for McKenna, but there is no response. There is a note left on the kitchen table for me:

Hey Luke, went out with Juliet. I'll be back soon.

I wish she hadn't gone out so that we could talk. The distance between us should never have grown. It is my fault for not hearing her out when I had the chance. I shouldn't have walked out. Even if she had lied to me, I should've allowed her to explain.

I am tired, so I take a shower and go to bed. Luka laid down on the floor next to me and went to sleep. I lied awake for a while, thinking about McKenna, replaying the memory of good times past, and fell asleep to the thought of her.

When I awoke the following day, she isn't beside me. I guess I had been too exhausted to wake up when she came home. I know she had because her side of the bed is still warm.

She'd probably already left for class. I am sorry I missed her, but today is the day Owen and I will finally face each other in the Proelium. I have to stay focused on that. No matter what McKenna and I are going through, there is no way she'd miss that fight, so I know I will see her later on tonight.

I make my way to Aurelius to prepare. I want to get down to the Arsenal and see if I can connect with my Origin again. The training room is packed with my brothers, all working on their skills, helping one another prepare. At least half of Aurelius's best fighters are scheduled to fight.

Down in the Arsenal, the fires of Aurelius burn as high and bright as always. I paid tribute to the mark of Aurelius and take up a position in the middle of the room. I close my eyes and begin to channel Spartacus. When we connect this time, the feeling is even more powerful. Every time I do it, I am amazed at how in tune I become with him. I am no longer myself when we connect.

We stay connected and train hard for about an hour. I check my phone as soon as it's time to take a rest. There is a missed voice message from McKenna. I waste no time listening to it:

I tried to wake you last night, but you were asleep, and again this morning, you wouldn't respond. I had to leave for class; if you wondered how come I wasn't there when you woke up. Luke, I miss you. I'm sorry I didn't tell you sooner about Owen and cried when you asked me. I felt guilty that I had lied to you and betrayed your trust. You should never have found out the way you did. What you should've known was that the day Juliet and I went out, I ran into Owen. He stepped in to protect me from this group of guys who were harassing me. That is all that happened. I wasn't having a secret relationship with him. He didn't even realize who I was at first. Owen thought I was just some damsel in distress. I should never have tried to hide it from you. Please come home to me before the fight tonight. I need to see you.

An overwhelming feeling of stupidity engulfs me. How could I have been so dumb as to allow my thoughts to get the best of me? I put the phone down and pick up my swords. I start flailing them around this time. I have lost focus, thinking about McKenna's message and the whole situation.

Out of the corner of my eye, I notice Shields watching me, leaning up against one of the support columns. "Getting carried away is not how you are going to have success with the sword. Don't think of it as a weapon--think of it as an extension of you. The sword is an entity. She is the reason your heartbeats, and you must be worthy of her greatness. You must dance with her, work as a single unit, and she will continue to honor you with glory far beyond what you could have ever imagined. She is the strongest part of you. So allow her to be."

"You make it sound as if the sword is alive," I say.

"Isn't she?" Shields replies. "McKenna is your sword. Never lose sight of that."

"How did you know I was thinking of McKenna?" I ask, wondering if he had overheard the message.

"Only a woman can give a man the kind of look that was on your face," Shields tells me. "Powerful creatures they are."

He is right as always: McKenna is my sword. I gather my things and run back to the car. I have to get home to her. On the way, I text her: *I'm on my way home to you.*

CHAPTER 11: OWEN

It's amusing to think that little runt truly believes he could take me in the arena. Luke, the Echo of Spartacus! How dare they call him the champion of Legacy? He's been here for three Proeliums, and all of a sudden, he's better than me? Ken was his only real test, and he has yet to meet a killer. From how he reacted to that statement about his whore, I can tell his mind is fragile and easily manipulated.

The meeting Lazarus had with Shields went better than expected. Who would've thought Shields could be stupid enough to offer his dog for slaughter? Three days from now, come the Proelium, Luke will become nothing more than a memory, just like his Origin. He dares face the great Owen, Echo of Achilles in battle? I guess his Origin wasn't smart enough to know when he had lost because Luke sure doesn't possess the intuition to do so.

After the meeting at the Sphere, we went back to the Crassus house. Lazarus is full of cheer after having gotten what he most yearned for. He wastes no time planning his next move.

"What a marvelous night!" Lazarus says to me. "The night of the Proelium will be one to remember for ages. Aurelius verse Crassus. Those feeble little fools will be lambs for the slaughter." Lazarus is sure that Crassus has the fight already won.

"The gods most certainly had a part in Shields' decision to sacrifice his best fighter in the Proelium. Why the goddess Fortuna has blessed us this evening. If it weren't for lack of effort from my long-since-dead ancestor Marcus Crassus, I wouldn't have to be the one to rescue the family name from shame and humiliation. He was not man enough to kill Spartacus, but I am."

"You seem to forget who will be the one to stand before a blade in the Arena," I say. "I will be the one to kill the Echo of Spartacus, not you."

"Oh, really. Shut up!" Lazarus barks. "You forget who is the namesake of this house. It is my name on which the foundation of this place was built, not yours. You'd do well to remember your place in this world."

"And where might that be?" I question. Lazarus has some balls to disrespect me like this. I pick up a letter opener on his desk in his office and point it at his throat.

"Where do you think it is? Calm yourself. No need to be so sensitive. Put that back where you got it... You're a god among men, Owen, a Titan who cannot be bested in the arena. But I am the God who has control over whether or not you are released to wreak havoc on the world."

"I am controlled by no man. I am no one's errand boy," Lazarus is sadly mistaken if he believes he can control me.

"Do you know what my vision is for the house of Crassus? My ancestors wished only to rank among the best of Legacy sects. I, on the other hand, have aspirations far beyond the arena. I would see this house elevated beyond the reach of any man."

"What are you talking about?" Even for him, this is delusional.

"What am I talking about? Immortality is what I'm talking about--starting with my Superior Legion, a collection of fighters rivaled by no other. I have located several Echoes scattered across the globe. Once I get rid of this Aurelius problem, nothing will stand between me and that glory."

"More Echoes? How did you manage to get that information? Goodwin was the only historian worth a grain of salt, and you had him killed."

Lazarus offered his annoying laugh. "Please. Goodwin refused my humble invitation to join me at Crassus. He was insignificant. Do you really think he was the only person capable of such knowledge? You could've spared his life," I am not opposed to killing, but only in the arena. There is a code, and in the arena, a man has a fair chance to fight for their lives.

"I could've spared his life? Oh, will you quit

already? Yes, I could've spared his life, but I chose to take it, just like the Bloodborn of Hector. His life could've been spared too, but you were instructed to do otherwise. Correct? So don't tell me no man controls you."

Lazarus continues describing his plan to become a god. Before he can finish, I've concluded I want nothing more to do with him.

He sees me shaking my head in disapproval. The gesture offends him.

"What is the matter now?" he asks.

"Lazarus, you are on a fool's mission far beyond your grasp. Taking a position next to the gods? Yeah, right. Focus your efforts on watching real men taste blood while you look on from your cozy box seat."

"What would you know of being a real man?" Lazarus asks.

"More than you."

"Please. I taught you how to fight and claim what you want with an iron fist and a sword. If it weren't for me, you would be nothing. Christ, I do not know what you want from me!"

"Sadly, I wish to only be your son, father. It baffles me how my mother ever stood you?" I stopped looking at him as my father a long time ago. He never cared for me, only for what I could do for him as the Echo of Achilles.

"I wish only to be your son," he says mockingly. "Grow a pair. You speak as if you have daddy issues. I never held you. So what? You are a Titan, nothing more, and you have no ambition beyond the arena. You fight me at every turn, never doing as I command. How did your mother stand me? How did I put up with her? You possess the same annoying qualities as she. That's why I shed no tears when I took her life. A son born from a mother whose legs I spread only so she could give birth to a seed of immortality!"

I am stunned and infuriated by his confession. I loved my mother dearly, and yet the memory of her had begun to fade from my thought. She died when I was a child. I never had the chance to say goodbye. The thing I remember so vividly is her voice, how she would hold me in her arms and rock me as she sang a song so sweet. She was with Lazarus the last time I saw her. He told me that he had put her to sleep and that she wouldn't be waking anytime soon. He said that I shouldn't worry about her. Time went on, and eventually, I stopped waiting for her to wake up. I never truly knew what became of her.

"You naive fool. Did you really think your mother has been asleep this whole time?" he asks. "I never loved your mother. When I searched for the bloodline of Achilles, I found her. Your mother was young and had no children of her own, so I took her as my wife. Not bad on the eyes, and I knew her offspring would be Bloodborn, so I blessed her with my seed. Pure Crassus blood, joined with the bloodline of Achilles, brought me you--Echo of Achilles." Lazarus is enjoying himself and his cruelty. "So pure and sweet, she was corrupting you from your purpose. I didn't want a nice little boy. I wanted a Titan! The only way to separate you two was to kill her--so I did. And thus, gave you the means to become the Titan who stands before me."

Lazarus is not a man; I can't believe that I was born

of a coward. Father or not, I will have his life soon.

"It's taken years and the price of blood, but now I see you for the man you really are. I will continue to fight under the House of Crassus but no longer embrace the name as my own. After the Proelium, go find yourself a new Titan. You'll get what you have coming to you one way or another. The gods won't let you go unpunished. And if they do, I'll kill you myself."

Being in his presence for so long has left a sick feeling in my stomach.

I go back to my apartment to find some peace. The loft I live in is still trashed from the night before. There are remains of food and red cups all over the place. My girlfriend Alexa had been home all day and hadn't lifted a finger to clean up. She is asleep in bed, her body covered just to the top of her perfectly curved buttocks by the tungsten-gray sheets, leaving her smooth bareback exposed. I sit beside her and wake her up.

She turns over, uncovering her head buried beneath a pillow, and brushes the wavy black hair from her eyes.

"Hi, babe," she says.

"Why is this place still a mess? What have you been doing all day?"

"Bad day?" she asks, closing her eyes and nestling her head back on the pillow.

"No more than any other."

"If you're worried about the Proelium, don't be. Trust your abilities," Alexa mumbles.

"Worried? I'm not concerned about Luke. He poses no threat. He's smaller and weaker than me."

"That's true," Alexa says, raising herself onto an elbow. "But he's no walk in the park either. He defeated Ken, and Baldr, and Erno as well. You would do well to not take him for granted."

I don't care to hear that. I grab a drink from the refrigerator. After the night I'd had, I figure I deserve one. Maybe even two. The thought of Lazarus killing my mother because he had found her bothersome is tormenting me. I can hear her screams and his pernicious laughter.

For the next two days, I have my cousin Kale

train with me away from the confines of Lazarus's prison. Kale is the Bloodborn of Ajax the Greater. He and I are the best fighters Crassus has to offer, close in age, and we'd been through a lot growing up together. We had been training with one another for as long as I can remember.

Kale is a brute in every sense of the word. He is about two inches taller than I am and considerably stronger. Kale lives to fight and never backs down from a challenge. He's never really cared much for his appearance--usually wearing his brown hair long and messy and hasn't shaved in years. What he lacks in skill and brains, he makes up for in an insatiable need for destruction. I had to keep him away from Crassus for the days leading up to the Proelium, so I can speak with him candidly.

"Are you ready for tomorrow night?" he asks.

"What's not to be ready for? You're the only person who stands a chance against me in the arena. The Echo of Spartacus-- I have no concern for him."

"Of course you don't!" Kale laughs."The sects of Legacy stand no chance against the likes of us. We will usher in a new era of power, crushing everyone who stands in our way."

He is confident in his vision.

"You'll have to do it without me, cousin."

The look on his face tells me he doesn't have a clue what I was talking about. "I have been commanded to fight for the name Crassus for far too long," I go on. "If I don't leave now, I'll end up killing Lazarus--my father and the man who took my mother's life."

Kale is stunned.

"Tomorrow, after the Proelium, I will part from Crassus and leave this world behind."

"I'll miss you, cousin," Kale says. He extends his hand to me, and we share a handshake out of respect. Lazarus doesn't need me to lead his vision, I think to myself. Kale is more than qualified for the job.

"I guess it must be comforting for you to know that, since you'll be gone, you'll no longer have to fight in my shadow, aye, little cousin?" He jokes.

We gather our things and leave the training grounds. In the car, I receive a phone call from Lazarus. "Is Kale with you?"

"Yes."

"Good. Come straight to my office. I need to discuss something with him."

I wonder what is so urgent but did as I was told. When we reach the office, Lazarus is sitting behind his desk with four other Crassus members. His minions, his go-to guys for anything he needs to be done that's dirty.

"Lazarus," asked Kale, "why have you called me here?"

"I need a favor. I want you to accompany these four gentlemen to the home of Luke and take care of his wife for me."

"What are you getting at?" I interject.

"With the Proelium approaching, I want to make sure that the Echo of Spartacus is not on his best game. I have no doubt that you will destroy him, but I'm taking no chances with my plans for domination so close in reach."

I feel my face go stiff. "Why do you need to do this? Luke is already in a weakened state because you had both Goodwin and Nikko killed." I'm having trouble holding back my anger. Why is Lazarus under the impression that I need help to defeat Luke? Is that why he'd had the others killed?

"Death comes in threes, my son," said Lazarus, chuckling. "I have no interest in your little rivalry with the man. This is not about you. You will do as I tell you. Destroy him and help me see this house elevated... Kale, take them to Luke's apartment and wait for his wife to be alone. Once Luke is gone, enter their home and kill her."

"Wait. Kale, stand down," I order. "I will do this," I tell Lazarus.

"You?"

"Yes. I have unfinished business with the woman. I will lead them right to her."

Lazarus seems skeptical but consents.

I don't want to do this, but I have no choice. If anyone is going to kill McKenna, it might as well be me. When the meeting is over, the five of us immediately make our way to Luke's apartment. We wait outside until morning when we finally see some movement. McKenna leaves first, early in the morning, followed by Luke a couple of hours later. We were instructed to kill her at home, so we have to wait some more until she returns. The longer we wait, the more irritated the minions are growing.

She finally appears. We get out of the car and approach as she is searching for her keys. I walk up behind her to create a distraction.

"Long time no see," I say.

McKenna is startled by my presence. "What are you doing here?" she asks frantically, looking around as if she is hoping there are witnesses.

That small interaction is all the time the others need to sneak up and grab her from behind. Three of them detain her while the fourth opens the door. No one is around to cause any trouble.

I do my best to keep her cooperative. McKenna knows the level of danger she is in, so it isn't hard for her to comply. Just in case she tried to yell, one of the minions kept her mouth muzzled. We forced her into the apartment. When we enter, she briefly eludes their grip and manages to bloody two of them. They secure her arms, and one of the two minions who had been punched returns the favor by striking her in the gut.

Their eyes grow wide with excitement. "Who wants to have a little fun with the girl before we kill her?" Someone asks.

"Yeah! Let's do her!"

"No one touches her!" I yell. "She will neither be violated nor killed. Is that clear? If any of you do otherwise, I will cut your hearts out. A few punches, and that's it! And if you speak a word of this to anyone, you're dead."

They start laughing and making noise. But just as the first hand rose to strike McKenna, a massive dog that looks like a wolf came flying from the bedroom hall and throws itself at him. In moments, the dog is tearing the fool to shreds.

A struggle ensues as McKenna tries to escape. She and the dog fight for their lives, giving everything they have for their survival. I look on in a daze as they punch and kick her. The sight of it makes me imagine my mother. I pictured her in McKenna's place on the floor. I admire McKenna's will; perhaps my mother had the same strength in her. Maybe she put up with Lazarus to protect me from him. I continue looking on until I can't stand to watch the assault anymore and force the men to stop. McKenna lay unconscious on the floor, blood seeping from her nose and dripping down the side of her mouth.

The dog stands over his wounded mother, baring his teeth. His bright red eyes glow even in the darkness of the apartment's shadows. Despite the situation, he doesn't show any fear. He stares at me, fully intending to make me his next victim. I don't want to harm him, but who knows what damage he might inflict if I am unsuccessful. Cautiously I move to strike, trying not to make any sudden movements. It seems as if he is mocking my actions. I ready myself, and the dog lunges to attack as soon as I flinch.

We race out of the apartment. The longer we stay, the greater the chance we have of someone coming by. We drive straight back to Crassus. Lazarus is waiting for us to return. The minions receive assistance from others who help carry the wounded inside.

"What happened to them?" Lazarus asks.

"Luke had a war dog in there that they were forced to deal with. The job is done, though. His wife is dead."

"Splendid! You have made me proud, son... Everyone, gather around!" He calls out. The house assembles, as he continues to speak, "tomorrow is the beginning of a new age in Crassus. After the Proelium, I will begin to set in motion my plan to control Legacy. Follow me, and together we will take our place among the gods! No sect will have the strength to deny us what we have been owed since birth. I have assembled you all from the greatest bloodlines the world has ever known. Your blood demands glory, and after tomorrow it will be ours!"

The speech is met with eager applause.

I don't share in their excitement. After what we had done, I want to be alone. I feel disgusted with myself.

It is only hours to the Proelium, and I have to get ready. I try to focus, but in the back of my mind, the vision of McKenna replays over and over. I never could have killed her; no part of me wanted to. I want to get as far away from the House of Crassus and Lazarus as possible.

I gather my things and leave for the Sphere. There are more people gathered for the night than I had ever seen before. They have come to see me destroy Luke in the arena, and I will not disappoint. When I feel the people's energy, I forget about the haunting images and set my mind to the most extraordinary battle anyone will ever see, Spartacus vs. Achilles. I hope Luke is ready because tonight will be his last!

CHAPTER 12: THE FINAL PROELIUM

There are still about nine hours until the beginning of the Proelium. I couldn't be any more prepared to fight. McKenna's voice message has really gotten to me. I regret ever getting mad at her in the first place. She wants to see me, and I can't get to her fast enough.

The drive back to the apartment has never seemed so long. I am so nervous to see McKenna. I don't know what I am going to say to her when I see her. Will I apologize and vow never to allow anything like this to come between us again? Or will I just take McKenna into my arms and embrace her because as long as I can hold her, I will always come home to her?

Walking down the hallway to the front door of our

apartment, I immediately sense a strangeness in the air. I get an overwhelmingly uneasy feeling. I look around, trying to figure out what is wrong when I spot a trail of blood leading to the stairs. I follow the drips and begin to grow nervous when I realize where they are heading. Close enough to see my door, I can tell it was left open. There is blood trickling down the white paint.

I rush inside, fearing the worst. When I push the door, Luka bares his teeth at me, growling. When he realizes who I am, he backs down. Luka is covered in blood. He is whining as he lay on top of McKenna, still trying to protect her. He returns to licking the wounds on her face and body.

I drop to the floor and scoop McKenna into my arms. I rub her sternum, trying to get her to wake up. When she finally comes to, I let out a massive sigh of relief. I pick her up off the floor and carry her into the bedroom. The apartment is in disarray. I know McKenna fought because I can see the signs of struggle. I can't believe this had happened. I lay her gently on the bed so that she would be comfortable.

McKenna is hazy as she regains consciousness. There is still blood trickling from her head. I went to the bathroom and got a wet towel so that I clean off her face.

"Luke, I'm sorry," McKenna says, mustering up the strength to speak.

"Stop apologizing. You did nothing wrong... I need you to tell me what happened."

"Owen. Owen showed up outside the apartment with four guys and forced their way in. They grabbed me and made me show them the way up here. I remember two of them talking about killing me, but Owen wouldn't let them. Luka did his best to save me; He was able to take out two of the guys. Owen eventually kicked Luka in the head and knocked him out."

This is all my fault. Thankfully McKenna was not killed, but I am enraged. My hands are shaking violently. I am fixating on Owen as I sit here covered in McKenna's blood.

Luka limps into the bedroom and sits at the bedside. I can't thank him enough for what he did. I got Luka to be with McKenna when I couldn't, but I never really thought that something like this would ever happen.

"I'm taking you to the hospital," I tell her.

"No. No hospitals. There'd be too many questions."

She is right.

My thoughts are swirling between her and the Proelium. Lazarus is going to pay. Owen alone was not responsible for what has taken place.

I stay with McKenna, nursing her for hours, while Luka sat on guard, watching the doorway and refusing to leave her side. McKenna had fallen asleep for a while but is starting to wake back up.

"What are you still doing here? You should have left by now."

"There's nowhere I have to be."

"Luke, I'll be all right. You have to fight Owen."

"How do you feel after sleeping?"

"I'm fine. I just have a headache, and I'm a bit sore. But I'm fine... While I was asleep, I had another dream. You were standing in the middle of the arena, watching as the crowd chant your name, praising you.

And there was a body at your feet."

"What do you think it meant?"

McKenna sits up to look me directly in the eyes. "Kill him!"

Her words light a fire in me. This is the opportunity I've been waiting for, and more importantly, McKenna wants him gone more than me. I stay with her for as long as possible. Eventually, her pain had diminished enough so that she was comfortable.

I compose myself before I leave the apartment. Gathering my thoughts so that I don't walk into the Sphere in a fit of rage. Lazarus may have successfully knocked me off my game, but I won't give him the satisfaction of seeing my emotion.

The parking lot of the Sphere is a madhouse when I arrive. People from all over have come for this once-in-a-lifetime event. The entrance line is longer than I've seen. I'm not even sure that the Sphere can house this many people. But they've chosen a goodnight to bear witness because this night of legends will set the tone for the future of Legacy.

I enter through a side entrance; I am not interested

in being hassled by the crowds. My Aurelius brothers are all here and ready for the battle. I see Shields outside the barracks and approach him to have a word.

"What happened?" he asks, noticing the bloodstains.

"Lazarus sent Owen and some men to my apartment this morning to kill McKenna. I found her shortly after we spoke in the Arsenal. She said that Owen wouldn't allow them to kill her, so they just severely beat her."

"I'm sorry," Shields says, with fury in his eyes.

"What do I have to do to get to Lazarus?" I ask.

"Stay focused on your fight with Owen. Once you have won in the arena tonight, Lazarus will be vulnerable, and Crassus will be at its weakest. You hold the power of vengeance on the tip of your blade. We'll only have one shot at how we go about this."

The walls of the Sphere begin to rattle as the crowd let us know of their praise. Great horns sound over the screams to signal the beginning of the Proelium. Shields shakes my hand gravely and disappears down the hall. I take a position in the shadows of the gates and watch as the first fight begins.

The Master of Ceremonies appears at the front of the solarium and addresses the crowd. "Ladies and Gentlemen, tonight we are blessed to witness a battle that would electrify the gods themselves. The Sphere is proud to host epic carnage between the houses of Crassus and Aurelius: four battles to boil your blood and strip the voices from your tongues. The last of the battles will brand a permanent place in your hearts. So, without further ado--let the Proelium commence!"

In moments, the first battle is underway. The crowd jumps to its feet as excitement courses through the bodies of every last soul in the audience. There is no shortage of blood--it is clear that Crassus has come to put on a show. The first Crassus fighter cut down my Aurelius brother as if he were carving a Christmas ham. It went the same way for the next battle. There will be no conceding tonight: Death is the only option.

Spirits are low after the first two battles. The five-man battle royal was up next, and Aurelius is growing weary. I can't allow them to enter the arena with low morale. Linc is fighting, and he will need everyone focused if he is to survive.

I enter the locker room and climb onto the table in the center of the room. "Brothers, lift your heads and focus your attention on me!" I demand. "I can see the concern for the next battle in your eyes. And if I can see it, so can those Crassus pigs! Save your sadness for after the Proelium because our slain brothers do not wish you to join them so soon. We are the only ones who can see that the deaths of our brothers do not go unpunished. I want you to taste the Crassus blood and bask in the glory as the crowd honors you by raining praise down upon your heads! Leave everything on the sand and take this night by the tips of your blades. For the brotherhood!"

"For Aurelius!" Everyone shouts.

I repeat the Aurelius mantra three times before leaping down from the table and leading the group out the door. I pat each man on the shoulder, as they shout back as if in one voice, once, twice, three times. I can sense that they are ready to take to the sand. Once again, the horns sound and the voice of the Master of Ceremonies broke through the deafening clamor. "Have you received enough blood?" he asks.

"No!" the crowd screams.

"Wonderful--because there is plenty more to be spilled in the battle royal!" The Master of Ceremonies points at both ends of the arena. The gates rise amid the din of stamping feet. Simultaneously, all ten fighters appear on the sand, the Crassus five in black and the Aurelius red.

Linc and Taylor lead the group for Aurelius, while Kale led Crassus. There is a brief pause as they size up one another. Then, Kale utters a great cry, and the fight explodes. Both sides charge ahead and collide in the center of the arena. A sharp shriek of blade against blade and the thump of chest armor booms when the warriors make contact.

Blood splatters all over the sand. The eerie sound of metal meeting flesh, and the sight of blood spraying the crowd, brought the battle so close to the audience they feel that they are in the match themselves.

Aurelius is fighting with courage and gradually gains the upper hand. One by one, the Crassus fighters begin to drop like flies. Linc, in particular, is fighting exceptionally well.

The odds are in Aurelius's favor--Kale is the only person left standing for Crassus, and we have three. However, he isn't going to give up without a fight. Linc and Taylor watch as Kale makes quick work of our teammate. Suddenly my two Aurelius brothers are left standing together to face the Bloodborn of Ajax alone.

They begin circling Kale, who attacks Linc first. Kale is exceptionally skilled at deflecting and dodging the Aurelius onslaught. Taylor lands the first blow, driving his blade into Kale's massive thigh.

He brushes off the wound and strikes Taylor in the face, sending him onto his back. Linc manages to slash the inner side of Kale's arm, which has weakened Kale once again.

Linc continues his attack, but Kale fends him off and punches Linc in the midsection. The power of the body shot doubles Linc over. He tries to get back up when Kale grabs him by the neck and lifts Linc's body off the ground. Linc dangles in the air, trying to break the man's grasp on his neck. I can see Linc wincing in pain as he struggling for breath.

Finally, Taylor rises from the ground, picking up his sword and driving it through Kale's leg, twisting as deep as he can into the flesh. Kale cries out as the tip of the blade emerges from the back of his thigh. Kale battles through the pain but releases his grip from Linc's neck.

As Linc falls to the ground, Kale turns his sights on Taylor. Kale rips Taylor away from his impaled sword; he grabs Taylor by the neck with one hand, and with the other, sends two sledgehammer size blows into Taylor's face. The second punch shatters Taylor's jaw and knocks him out cold.

Linc musters enough energy to get back on his feet, and he launches himself at Kale's head. Landing a dropkick that sends the giant to the ground. Linc capitalizes by racing to pull the sword from Kale's leg, sending a stream of blood spurting across his face as he sticks the blade's point against Kale's throat.

"Choose," Linc growls.

Kale lifts his hand, giving the sign for life. Kale has chosen to live, and Linc honors his request.

The crowd is elated as Linc thrusts up his arms in victory. I glance up at the solarium during the celebration. Lazarus's face has grown anxious. His facial expression has made me happy. I want him to suffer.

The man had tried to rip the beating heart from my chest. There is only one way to repay his treacheries.

My heart is pounding as I stand before the arena entrance, eager for the gate to rise. The crowd is stomping their feet--boom, boom, pow, boom, boom, pow. The rhythmic pounding grows louder still. Finally, the Master of Ceremonies comes to the front of the solarium once more. He raises his voice to be heard.

"The gods smile upon us tonight, for we are blessed to witness a battle that could have only been forged by their hands--a battle of Titans that will in time become a storied legend, to be verified as truth only by those privileged to have witnessed. Those of you here tonight! The greatest warrior the world ever saw, Achilles, blesses us from the afterlife with his Echo Owen, the bringer of death--to face the champion of

Legacy, Luke the Echo of Spartacus!"

The gates rise, and the sound of chains clanking rings in my ears.

Owen enters the arena first, as the crowd greets him with frightful applause. There is no one standing between us now.

As I take my first steps onto the sand and hear the crowd scream my name as I had dreamed, I remove the cuirass from my chest to expose McKenna's dried blood still on my flesh. I wore a black sleeve on my left arm fashioned with buckles from the shoulder to the wrist. I take my position in the center of the arena and acknowledge the crowd, the red shroud fastened securely to my right hand.

The Master of Ceremonies yells out, "Begin!" and the battle is immediately underway.

Owen and I trade blows for a while, neither one of us landing any strikes. As ready as I have been leading up to the fight, my body is fighting without me.

I release a piercing howl as Owens's sword opens a six-inch gash in the right side of my rib cage. The wound sends me straight to my knees. But after that initial moment, I can no longer feel the pain. My mind is in another place, and I have to admit it doesn't bother me. I glance down at the warm blood coursing from my body and can see what appears to be a rib in the center of the large wound I have sustained.

The only thing that matters to me right now is how I couldn't fail McKenna. Those Crassus dogs would never have gotten to her if I had been with her. Being away from her is killing me, but I will not allow Owen to get away with what he had done.

"Get up!" I grunt. An adrenaline rush ignites every atom of my body.

I rise to my feet with a renewed vigor. The look in my eyes speaking of my intent.

A grin breaks across my face as I take a knee on the sand. I can't help but smile at the thought of Owen assuming he has already won this match.

"Is that all you've got?" I ask.

"I am surprised. You are not without skill," Owen admits. "But you were stupid to have risen. I was going to allow you to lie there and bleed out--you know, as I did that tasty little whore of yours. Now I'm going to have to make sure you don't get back up," said Owen.

"Too bad for you, she didn't die. Just so you know, I'm done holding back!" I reply.

Shields once told me that, to be a truly great fighter, a great gladiator, one had to be able to separate one's human nature from the animal inside: *"Whenever you fight, mercy must not exist! If a man chooses to step in the arena with you, there's only one option. Win if you want to live. Do whatever it takes to survive!"*

I glance up into the crowd again, watching them cheer as our blood paints the sand. Scanning the thousands of screaming faces, my eyes stop on one. It's McKenna she's here. She gathered up her strength and found her way to the Sphere. She had promised never to miss a fight, and she is keeping her promise. McKenna has fought death to be with me.

My focus has just become unbreakable. I get a second wind as my strength returns, and I rise to my feet. I feel my heart begin to pound heavily as Spartacus comes through and takes over my body.

Owen advances at me with an assortment of moves I quickly avoid, and as I back away, I land an unexpected reversing strike across his abdomen. The blow weakens him. I can tell and immediately begin to move on the offensive. I start attacking with a blind ferocity. Owen blocks all that he can but is unable to keep himself from getting carved up.

I kick Owen on the side of his knee and hear a loud crack as it hits the ground. He is in shock and, while his guard is down, in one continuous motion, I shove my left blade through his chest.

The crowd gasps as I am standing over a kneeling Owen holding a sword wedged in his chest. A wide-eyed look comes over him as the life drains from his face.

"Well done," he grimaced. "You have bested me."

I stare at him with a neutral gaze. "I promised you the next time we saw each other, I would kill you. I have kept my promise. Enjoy death."

Owen hunches over as his body grows weak. With the breath fading from his mouth, Owen lets out a hushed laugh and says, "All men meet their end. Only the time and the manner differ. I am happy to see the afterlife."

He raises his head up and looks at the night sky visible through the giant glass roof over the arena. With my right hand, I lift my sword and drive it across his neck. His severed head flies off as blood rains heavily upon the sand, his body slumps forward and crash to the ground with a sickening thud.

The crowd is overcome. They chant Spartacus, Spartacus, Spartacus, as I stand over Owen's body and raise my hands in victory.

I look up and see Lazarus' face pale and eyes dark with fury. He is staring at me, and I am glaring right back. I know this will not be the last time we look each other in the eye.

Out of nowhere, a black-hooded figure appears like a reaper behind Lazarus. He turns noticing the strange feeling of Death whose come to collect. Face to face with this apparition Lazarus freezes unable to move out with fear having set in. Suddenly, a woman sitting in the solarium lets out an eardrum-shattering scream as Lazarus's body falls to the ground before her like a tree.

The crowd frantically begins to scurry out of the

Sphere as Security chases after two other hooded figures running in opposite directions. I don't know what is going on--the crowd is in a panic and a new threat has entered the arena.

I look back at the solarium and notice the hooded figure jump to the sand trying to escape. A concealed extension knife is fastened to his arm. The man removes a bottle from his cloak pocket and begins pouring a liquid on the pitch. I can't make out the symbol he is drawing until he takes out a lighter and drops it on the ground. The liquid he had dispensed was some sort of ignition fluid that has burst into flames in an "S" shaped symbol.

The man doesn't stay around to watch the fire burn. Instead, he slips into the crowd and is quickly out of sight. Whoever has attacked Lazarus has left a calling card for the crime. He wants everyone to know exactly who it was that has ended Crassus.

CHAPTER 13: THE LAST MESSAGE

McKenna has been healing nicely, two weeks have gone by, and her bruises have all almost disappeared. Only a faint scar is left on the upper part of her forehead near her hairline.

I am still grateful to Luka for protecting McKenna. Maybe I should start training him in bite work. I don't want to put him in danger either, but if he is willing to put his life on the line, he might as well be prepared for anything if it were to happen again.

"Any news about the stabbing?" she asks.

"None that I've heard...yet. I'm going to meet Shields today at Aurelius. I'll see if he's learned anything."

"I can't say that I'm not happy it happened to him," McKenna says. "He deserved it. I just wonder who those hooded people were."

I had the same question--that, and how they'd found the most opportune time to strike Lazarus down. I have my suspicions, but I am not going to start any rumors. If my suspicions are correct, it would explain a lot of unanswered questions I have.

"Hey, I've wanted to ask you something," she says.

"Go on."

"The night of the Proelium, you gave me this indescribable look. It was almost like you had an epiphany. What were you thinking?"

"When I saw you sitting in the crowd, bruised and battered, the image of you lying in my arms shook me. My promise was broken--harm had met you at our door, and I was not there to protect you. All I kept thinking to myself when I found you was, please don't let her be dead. I would have had to find you in the afterlife because there would no longer have been any reason to go on living."

"No, you wouldn't do that."

I shake my head. "What use is my heart without you to give it meaning? I would slay the world to be by your side."

"Then the world should be grateful for my survival," McKenna replies.

I leave the apartment and go meet Shields. The meeting isn't going to be long. McKenna and I have plans.

When I get to his office, the door is open. I knock anyway.

"Come in, Luke," he says. Shields is seated behind his desk with the back of his chair turned away from the door. I can't help but notice the papers scattered on the desk. A manila envelope lay on top of the pile. All of the documents have letterheads with the same burning symbol from the arena. I see the word Shade beneath one of the documents.

"What is this?" I ask Shields.

"It is what it looks like. You remember when Goodwin said he had to retrieve something important the night he was stabbed? This was it."

"So you--"

"Yes. I am a member of Shade. Goodwin was a part of helping create the new order."

I almost don't believe what I am hearing. I thought the legend of Shade was as old as the identities of the Assembly council. So what does Shields have to do with it?

"What is Shade?" I ask.

"A secret order of Legacy restorers. Have you ever heard of the Knights Templar?"

"Yes, of course."

"With impending war on the rise, the Catholic church searched for a blessing from God so that its warriors would be victorious in battle. That came in the form of the Knights Templar--created by Pope Callixtus II in 1119, a descendant of an original Shade affiliate. So that he wouldn't bring attention to Legacy, he called the newly inspired order the Knights Templar. Beyond that, many groups were formed over the years, names were changed, but they always had the same agenda.

"Goodwin had been watching Lazarus's movements for a long time. When he found out that

Lazarus's affiliation with the Assembly went further than we first thought, we decided that, for the sake of Legacy, a new order had to be formed. We knew that Lazarus would, as the leader of the Assembly, see to the destruction of Legacy."

"Why are you telling me this?" I ask.

"Because Lazarus did not die at the Proelium."

"So you were the one I saw fleeing from the solarium?"

"Yes. The Proelium was the perfect place to attack. Once you finished Owen, I knew that Lazarus would be too distracted to notice the impending danger. We had people in the crowd waiting for me to give the signal the entire night. I was supposed to assassinate Lazarus and send a message to the Assembly that Shade was back and coming for blood.

"Thomas wanted to tell you together, when the time was right, about the order, but Lazarus got to him before that could happen. Lazarus was counting on Owen to end you that night. Now that he has survived, he's hell-bent on changing history once again, and he'll be coming for you and this house harder than ever."

I don't quite know what to say. I thought the man had been killed then and there when his body fell.

"Word around the Legacy community," Shields goes on, "is that Lazarus is now in power. Sects are already talking about disbanding for fear of his rule. It will no longer be about sport in Legacy. Lazarus will try to dictate the outcomes of the Proeliums, and if that happens, no fighter will be safe. Legacy will collapse, and the destruction of this world will commence."

I am shocked by what I am hearing. I imagine all the blood that would run at the hands of Lazarus. Something needs to be done, and it appears that Shields has already begun to do it. I look at the papers once more. The top one, in particular, caught my attention.

"What is this?" I ask him, picking up the sheet I had been eying.

"The last thing Thomas did for us before he died. The night after the meeting with Lazarus, I went by the hospital to see Thomas. I told Thomas that the first phase had begun, and he handed me a list, a roster of Echoes that he and Bobby had been gathering. What you're holding in your hand is that list. It contains the profiles of those Echoes, their names, and their whereabouts.

"Thomas, always thinking ahead, knew that if the plan backfired in any way, we would need to gather new fighters to defend Aurelius against Lazarus's Superior Legion. And, unfortunately, it did when Lazarus survived. Owen was supposed to lead Lazarus's group. Now Lazarus has acquired someone new, who has somehow located five of the worst kinds of Echoes imaginable.

"Thomas's list consists of three Echoes who will complement this brotherhood well enough to stop Lazarus. With malevolence building up in Legacy, Aurelius will look to their champion to lead them out of the darkness and into a new age."

With Nikko gone, I have assumed the mantle as leader of the brothers. Shields is correct; with Lazarus in power, the fate of everyone in Legacy is in danger. I will not see this house fall and its brothers stripped of life to indulge a psychopath's ego. Too much blood has been wastefully spilled. For the brotherhood and my wife, I will raise my swords and stand before a thousand men.

Immortality is found in those who genuinely care for us. Owen was not a demigod; neither was his Origin. Men who meet death early in life live on as legends, but warriors who face battle and live to see old age become divine in the afterlife. We can't live forever. We are all human, and our humanity gives birth to extraordinary lives. Eventually, our clock will run down, but until then, we are blessed to live as boundless men who choose how we meet our end. I choose to live, to love my wife unconditionally in this life for as long as the heart beats beneath my chest, and when the time presents itself, follow her to the afterlife. I choose to live, to defend Aurelius's honor and my life from the next person who tries to take it. I was right when I questioned if there was someone in death who sought after me. I just didn't know their name. My journey and this fight for freedom are just beginning. The people call me the champion of

Legacy, but, I am, Spartacus!

EPILOGUE

The Edge of the Abyss

He clenches his fists, trying to steady himself. "Really think about it," he whispers hoarsely, "we're summoning a cataclysm. If we fail..." His voice fractures like a column under the pressure of the world's weight.

Once a vibrant warrior, he now wears an expression as grave as a tombstone. He stands at a grand window, the night outside as dark as their prospects. Slowly, he turns, his eyes a storm of their own. "And if we succeed," he replies, his words laced with a bitter venom, "we'll be standing amidst the wreckage of our own lives. But perhaps, just perhaps, we'll have saved the world."

"Reviving Shade...," he stutters, "it's not just playing with fire. It's diving into an inferno. We will be renegades, hunted like dogs by everyone—Legacy, Crassus, the world."

"We will be renegades," he hisses, "but isn't it the destiny of a renegade to slay a monster before it devours everything?"

Trembling now, his fear is almost a tangible entity in the room. "Lazarus is a demon in the guise of a man. His vision of a modern Roman Empire... it's a poison that will seep into the veins of society. It's already beginning."

"That," he replies, saying each word deliberately and sharp as a blade, "is exactly why he needs to die. Before the world is forced to kneel at his feet."

"And if we fail," he rasps, his anxiety like a vice gripping his chest, desperately inhaling as if each breath might be his last. "If he uncovers our plot..."

Turning back to his fearful accomplice, a thousand-yard stare ignited with an almost feral intensity. "Then we fail fighting," he growls. "I'd rather die on my feet than live in a world suffocated by a tyrant."

Inspired by the words spoken by his stalwart companion, he takes a deep breath, calming his nerves. Soon his voice steadies and becomes ironclad.

"Then we will not fail," he declares. "Shade will rise from the shadows and sever the serpent's head before it strangles the world."

Silently, Shields extends a hand, placing it firmly on Goodwin's shoulder—a gesture of unity in their perilous pact. In a voice that is almost a prayer, he whispers, "In this desperate hour, we are the world's last, fraught hope."

Their shared gaze is a collage of resolve and fear, as they knowingly gamble with everyone's lives, stepping closer to the edge of an abyss from which there might be no return.

Here, in this moment, suspended like matter devoid of gravity, they accept the risky path they've chosen, knowing that success may lead to their salvation—or failure, the accelerant to a cleansing fire the likes of which the world has never seen.

SCAN THE QR CODE FOR A
SPECIAL MESSAGE FROM J
LEONARD COSTNER

ABOUT THE AUTHOR

J Leonard Costner

A Pen that Paints Worlds

Born in America but shaped by Europe, J Leonard Costner's life has been as varied and vibrant as the characters in his novels. An artist by trade and a former athlete, Costner infuses his unique experiences and perspectives into every page he writes.

Raised across the grand tapestry of Europe, Costner grew up amidst an array of cultures, languages, and histories that would later breathe life into his stories. His upbringing gave him an appreciation for the rich complexities of people and places—an appreciation that shines through in his work.

Transitioning from a celebrated career in sports, Costner found his next calling in 2012: storytelling. His debut series, "Legacy", is a testament to his boundless creativity. Intricately weaving history with fantasy, and reality with myth, Costner's works are as much a vivid painting as they are compelling narratives. His words aren't just read; they are experienced. Each chapter, a stroke of paint on a grand canvas.

Costner's writing style is as unique as his life journey. With an academic background in art, he writes to illustrate—each sentence crafted not just to tell a story, but to show it. He shapes each scene with the meticulous care of a painter, choosing his words with the precision of a brushstroke.

In "Legacy", and in all of his works, Costner invites readers not just into a story, but into a world. A world that is at once enchanting and believable, vast in scope but intimate in emotion.

Today, J Leonard Costner continues to write, each new work a labor of love, a new landscape painted with words. He is not just an author, but an artist of narrative, a craftsman of worlds, and a guide for readers looking for an adventure that defies the ordinary.